First published in Great Britain in 2007 by Comma Press
3rd Floor, 24 Lever Street, Manchester M1 1DW
www.commapress.co.uk

'The Dogs' was first published in *The Guardian,* 17 July 2004. 'The Deadly Space Between'
first appeared in *Phantoms at the Phil II* (Northern Gothic / Side Reel Press, 2006).

A CIP catalogue record of this book is available from the British Library

ISBN 1-905583-07-9
EAN 978-1-905583-07-2

The publishers gratefully acknowledge assistance from the Arts Council England
North West, as well as the support of Literature Northwest.

www.literaturenorthwest.co.uk

Set in Bembo by XL Publishing Services, Tiverton
Printed and bound in the United States of America.

PHOBIC

Modern Horror Stories

Edited by
Andy Murray

For Nigel Kneale
for keeping the form alive.

CONTENTS

CONTENTS

Introduction

The things you're scared by can be very subjective. I vividly remember as a kid of about six going to visit my cousin Mike who lived a few minutes' walk away. He had a story LP, called something like 'Noddy and the Witch'. We sat up in his room listening to it, transfixed by the screeching, cackling voice of the witch, staring at the illustration of her on the back of the album. Thereafter I was petrified at the very prospect of going back to that house. I didn't even like walking past it. I'd peer fearfully up at Mike's bedroom window and think, 'That thing's still up there!' Even today, I get a shudder when I go near Acresfield Road. My relatives don't even live there any more. Silly, really. Entirely irrational. But that's being scared for you. It's subjective.

Sharper minds than mine have long since noted that horror as a genre is most effective when, either by design or by accident, it taps into the collective unconscious. When Western society was alarmed by the ambitions of science, it brought forth *Frankenstein*. A few years after the end of the First World War, Universal began their horror film cycle, mirroring the West's repulsion at this wholesale bloodshed, by bringing forth supernatural beings from literature and folk-tales, and assorted menaces – to both catch and contain this new fear. Hammer Studios pulled off a similar trick in the wake of the Second World War. Indeed throughout the twentieth century, popular culture plundered collective anxieties about the bomb, modern medicine, and the depersonalising Red Peril as fuel for film, fiction and TV: *The Thing from Another World* (1951), *Invasion of the Bodysnatchers*

(1956) and *Doctor Who*'s Cybermen being just three examples. But times change. The world we're living in is very different to that which even our parents were born into. All of which raises the question: what are today's collective fears and anxieties, and how can an updated genre tap into them?

This anthology is made up of various writers' responses to the question. Many of the authors here are established and award-winning figures. Among their number are screenwriters, comic writers, playwrights and novelists. Some are new to prose, and many are new to the horror genre. This is entirely intentional: we wanted to create an anthology both broad in scope and fresh in approach. All we asked was that the stories be contemporary in setting and in feel; and that they unsettle us.

The stories collected here cover a wide range of responses. Some are dark; some are satirical; some near-psychedelic. Each one circumvents the weary, clichéd trappings of bad horror. Instead of the denizens of Hell or the lurching undead, these tales are anchored in recognizable modern life. Where the supernatural world shows its face, it's merely as a fleeting intimation.

What's truly fascinating is the way in which these 15 varied stories nevertheless dovetail and overlap. Our modern world is steeped in technology, and here the latest manifestations of it – mobile phones, email, chat-rooms, home security systems – are imbued with a hint of lurking menace. Contemporary city life figures heavily, too. There's as much urban unease, obsession and madness as paranormal activity in the stories that follow. In our cynical, secular world, it seems we've got as much to fear from things hiding in dark corners at the end of the street as we have from the eternal hereafter.

There's also a strong preoccupation with the safety of loved ones, especially children. A timeless fear at heart, but a particularly rejuvenated one at present. It would appear that, in the new millennium, the simplest things – the most innocent and fragile things – are the ones that affect us deeper than ever. Horror exists to take all these anxieties and to project them, extrapolate from them, until the ordinary threatens to break through into the extraordinary. Just as a sad song might give us a peculiar boost on a miserable day, horror stories can put our fears into black and white, magnify them, and enable us to come to terms with them.

There are certainly two distinct paths open to the modern horror author. One is to identify classic fears – those that have been mined for fiction and films since time immemorial – and present them afresh for a new generation. In this camp, Ramsey Campbell has long been acknowledged the master, terrifying modern audiences with his sorcery of the seemingly familiar. His story here 'Digging Deep' is no different, refreshing that age-old nightmare of being buried alive. Frank Cottrell Boyce's 'The Part of Me That Died' also breathes new, unexpected life into a well-worn horror trope – namely the sinister, animated inanimate object; whilst with 'The Coué', Jeremy Dyson reconfigures MR James' 'Passing the Runes' for the world of eBay and chat-rooms.

A different approach emerges in Matthew Holness' 'Sounds Between', which depicts a contemporary London shadowed by the threat of suicide bombings and a distant war. Likewise Maria Roberts' 'By the River' imagines a near-future just beyond the climate change headlines. This second option forgoes the temptation to reawaken classic fears in favour of entirely new preoccupations. Some stories manage to blend both approaches, like Paul Magrs' 'The Foster Parents' which takes an age-old myth and re-forges it in the suburban curtain-twitching paranoia of two *Daily Mail* readers. You could argue Robert Shearman's closing story stands the entire genre on its head.

But do any of these stories actually re-invent horror? Of

course not. The boldest claim we could make for them is they observe a tradition — that of pitching up unearthly elements into ordinary settings — with only the ordinary in need of reinvention. The stories here are honest, imaginative, vivid, and varied. They're not mechanical in their desire to unsettle, but personal to their authors and occasionally genuinely strange.

Fear, after all, is subjective.

Sounds Between

MATTHEW HOLNESS

'Who's it smiling at?'

It *was* smiling. An ugly slash of paint smeared itself between each burst of mirrored sunlight. When at last the balloon settled and twisted back in his direction, a movement barely noticeable in the still summer air, Philip perceived a crudely drawn face.

'You,' he said, rubbing away sleep.

'Wrong,' answered Mary. 'I think it wants you.'

'Not my type.' Philip smiled back at the strange head hanging motionless in the sky beyond their bedroom window. The balloon was one of the helium-filled kind; two sheets of aluminium foil sealed together roughly along a plastic seam. The primitive features daubed across its front, two eyes above an upturned mouth, formed a black stain upon its reflective lining. Below dangled a grubby length of coloured string. The balloon dipped suddenly as it began to lose buoyancy.

'He's on his way out,' Philip said. 'Not a single friend to hold his hand. Must be his lack of personality.'

'He's going down like one of your jokes,' said Mary as the bathroom door slammed shut, closing him off from her private rituals. Philip opened the window, listening for distant sirens. Outside the air felt even more humid as the balloon sank lower, wilting visibly in the heat. Mary re-emerged, half-dressed, eating an apple.

'Move,' she said, nudging Philip away from the bed as she finished drying her hair. He watched her until she grew uncomfortable and slapped his leg.

'Don't stare,' she said, glancing at the bedside clock. 'I'm not an object.'

'There's a small line running down the side of your face where you've been sleeping,' he said. 'It's cute.' He reached across to stroke her cheek as she pulled away.

'What's today, then?' Mary asked. 'More tasteless laughs at the innocent?'

'I'm working on the programme again, if that's what you mean.'

'With him?'

'With him.'

'Shouldn't you save room for a nice cosy breakfast for two, then?'

Philip continued pouring coffee. 'No, he was at an awards party last night.'

'He's probably dropping some poor girl at a tube right now,' said Mary. 'Shame she doesn't have my willpower, or a knight in shining armour at her side.' From her expression Philip suspected he had begun to blush.

'Why so early?' he said, following her into the hall. 'Why not leave it half an hour?'

'I have a proper job. Unlike you funny boys, I don't have the luxury of choosing when I do it.'

'Can't you start late then work late?' he said, feeling embarrassed in his pyjamas. 'That way you'd miss rush-hour.'

'Me and everyone else,' Mary replied, unlocking the front door. 'Anyway, a stranger walks into my life today and changes everything. You'd best hang on tight if you want to keep hold of me.'

She paused.

'Are you going to tell me what it is?'

'What do you mean?' Philip replied, wondering whether or not she had found the film.

'You tell me. You're the one not getting any sleep.'

Philip decided she hadn't, and shook his head.

'See you at lunch.' Mary's voice was cold. 'Good luck with the recording. I'm sure it'll be hilarious. Just remember they're buying something from you. It might feel like money for nothing, but you're giving them what *they* want.'

'And talent has nothing whatsoever to do with it?' he snapped. The question went unanswered as Mary stepped out into the stairwell. Philip noticed she was wearing the scarf. Instantly, he saw her a year ago, waving up to him from the courtyard outside, oblivious to what horrors awaited her later that morning.

'Don't wear that,' he said, before he could stop himself.

'I'll see you at two. Give Alec a kiss from me.'

'Be careful on the tube.'

She avoided his lips and descended the stairs. Philip watched the back of her head bobbing downwards as if tugged by something beneath. Then he ran to the kitchen window in time to catch her final wave from below; a daily ritual that now merely mimicked the scene etched more permanently upon his memory. It played endlessly inside his mind, changeless and inescapable; like the film he'd been sent of the dying man. The man killed in the desert, crushed under a grinding vehicle.

Philip switched on his computer when he was sure Mary would not return, and deleted the small media file that kept appearing at the corner of his screen. Maybe this time it would disappear. The sound of sirens rescued him from recalling what sights it contained, drawing him towards ominous shots of emergency service teams floundering in the streets of the capital. He reached over and switched off the television, silencing the archive footage that seemed to have run continuously throughout the year.

Confirming that the file was indeed sitting in his waste basket, Philip erased it again with a click of his mouse, glancing instinctively over his shoulder. Through the window, some distance away, the balloon watched. Philip could just make out the blurred smudge of its features, running like polluted streams across its silver face. Without warning, it rose slowly into the air.

'Fraud,' he said, and waved it goodbye.

He wasn't told what the problem was until the fast service to London passed a second time, and even then the message was unclear. Points failure wouldn't explain the heavy police presence visible at each station, and if Philip had overheard the guards correctly, 'searches' were being conducted throughout the morning on trains operating along this route. Wondering if anyone had yet moved into his carriage from behind, he turned to find it empty. Not unusual this late on a weekday morning, he reassured himself.

The train slowed to another premature halt. Through the window a drab stretch of terraced houses lined the route into West Hampstead station. A huge St. George's Cross hung as usual below its grimy ground floor window, groping towards the earth through a garden of broken furniture and household rubbish; its white fabric spotless.

The sound of a low-flying helicopter slowly separated itself from that of a lone bluebottle battling glass. Philip scanned the sky overhead as the whirring of rotor blades faded; they returned moments later as the helicopter began circling his location.

Human shouts carried themselves down from somewhere further up the line, muffled by the persistent electrical hum of the train's engine. Philip checked the bin behind his seat. It contained nothing but discarded coffee cartons and newspapers. The luggage rack above him was also clear. A text message arrived from Mary, and as Philip opened it he froze.

The cold familiar wash of adrenaline swept through him as he re-read her desperate plea from a year ago, the raw terror of her words retaining their ability to shock. Philip closed the message down, but did not delete it, surrendering once more to an irrational belief he had yet to shake off; that were he ever to destroy Mary's helpless cry, the private deal struck between himself and whatever powers had granted her life that day would end. How and why the message had been sent to him again, meanwhile, remained unclear.

As it passed through West Hampstead station, the train began to pick up speed. The platform was deserted, and Philip glimpsed police tape barring the station entrance at the stairway overlooking the railway line. As a loud wail of vehicle sirens screamed along West End Lane, his world plunged into darkness.

Echoes of alarms grew more frantic as they traversed the wide stretch of tunnel sprawling toward Kentish Town. When the train finally re-emerged into daylight the sirens were joined by others from various directions. Philip caught sight of the helicopter, far above and shimmering brightly in the morning sunshine.

Moments later he stepped out onto an empty platform, making for the stairs leading to the station exit where a fellow passenger had already begun the slow climb upwards.

'Bit hot for that, isn't it?' commented the station official as Philip approached the barrier.

'Sorry?' he said, presenting his ticket.

'Not you,' the man replied. 'That one, all togged up for rain.'

Philip glanced ahead at the figure now exiting the station, catching the back of a sheeny raincoat attached at its neck to a wide and floppy-looking hood, which seemed to inflate as it encountered a sudden downwind.

'Might turn, I guess,' the man finished, waving Philip through. 'Could do in a flash.'

'Has anything happened?' said Philip, fumbling for his mobile as a new message announced itself. 'I thought I heard sirens. Somewhere nearby.'

'Not that I know of,' the man replied.

Crew, unapologetic, failed to suppress his laughter.

'Who did send it, then?' demanded Philip, pacing the street outside Kentish Town, struggling to hear his producer's voice against the constant rush of traffic. He winced at the thought of it touching his ear; the vile image sent to his phone that had somehow sealed itself instantly as a permanent background.

'I didn't think mobiles got viruses,' he said.

'Oh they do, believe me,' said Crew in smooth, pleasant tones. 'It's all those dirty numbers you must be calling.'

'It's the same thing you sent me in the email,' Philip countered. 'The dying soldier. It's from the same bit of film.'

'I said I wouldn't send you any more, didn't I?'

Philip pictured Crew's smile; controlled and unshakeable.

'Didn't I?'

'Yes,' he answered.

'So get off the phone, Philip, save your hard-earned cash and *run* to the studio where Alan and I are still waiting for you to begin this one in a million job you've spent so many of your precious years working towards, and I'll personally sort it out when you get here. Deal?'

'Okay. Just, please...'

'Philip, you are late, and you're not A-list yet.' Crew's interruption was polite yet firm, and with an inexplicably jovial goodbye, he hung up. Philip made his way up a side street to avoid the crowds milling about the pedestrian crossing, tempting traffic, and opened the message again to re-check the identity of the sender. Shielding his phone from the view of others, he scrolled down past the grainy image of the burst head. Below, in the space where a name or number should have appeared, the same tiny graphic symbol remained.

A smiling face.

Philip tried once more to delete it.

The dark, cramped booth contained nothing but a microphone, chair and small playback screen. Philip tucked a pile of DVDs he'd expressed interest in at last week's script read-through beneath his seat.

'Courtesy of the production budget,' Crew had declared with a wink while ushering him inside, the habitual smile appearing somewhat stiff through one night's stubble and yesterday's suit.

Visible through a large pane of sound-proofed glass, the producer now sat behind the mixing desk with a technician called Alan, who directed Philip's attention toward the headphones slung over one corner of the display.

'Phil or Philip?' Alan asked once Philip was wearing them.

'Phil,' interrupted Crew from the right earpiece. 'Phil Dobson, Hackney stand up award finalist... three years ago?'

'Four,' Philip corrected him.

'Four,' confirmed Crew.

'Did you win?' asked Alan.

'Joint third.'

The sound link to the studio cut out as the two men laughed openly. Alan's voice then returned.

'Belated congratulations.'

'Sorry I was late,' Philip said. 'I didn't see a sign or anything outside.'

'Sorry we're not some flashy Soho studio.'

'I didn't mean...'

A painful blast of feedback pierced Philip's ears.

'Apologies,' said Alan, his distorted voice fading as the volume input lowered dramatically. Muffled sniggering accompanied its return.

'Technically that's a violation of health and safety. I have just been reliably informed that you are within your rights to sue me.'

Philip attempted a smile as Crew appeared at the door.

'This footage isn't actually finished,' he explained. 'You haven't seen any of it yet. It's a rough edit, but what we need you to do is make up some funny stuff over the top to see if it'll work. Alright?'

'Sure.'

'It's due for Friday's show, so we need to press on at pace.'

'Okay,' Philip agreed, examining the playback screen lit up in front. On it was frozen an infra-red image.

'Night camera footage,' declared Crew with a hint of pride. 'Have a quick watch, and we'll go for one straight away.' The door shut tight behind him.

'Okay, here's the playback,' said Alan as the screen came to life.

The scene was a desert waste-ground. Tiny white silhouettes ran frantically in various directions, throwing themselves against walls and objects. Spitting out from the bottom of the camera came rows of lightning fast projectiles, which Philip soon identified as tracer fire from a military vehicle. Amid the bizarre devastation, Philip followed one rather prolonged game of cat and mouse in which a man ducked desperately from bullets raining down upon him, eventually escaping into a hidden cave mouth. Viewed like this, the scene resembled a primitive computer game.

Next door's laughter emerged through the connecting microphone.

'Okay, here we go.'

'Sorry, can I ask something?' said Philip.

'Fire away,' said Crew.

'Is this… what is this?'

'Hold on, hold on.'

Crew swept past the window separating them and wrenched open the door.

'This is simply a small thing we're putting in over the end titles. We just need voiceover. Anything, really. Improvise.'

'Isn't it a bit inappropriate?'

'This is a satirical show, Philip. It's your job to make it funny.'

'But…' Philip hesitated, then continued. 'You're the producer. You must have some idea.'

'Make it funny. That's the idea.' Crew shrugged his shoulders and left. Philip's eyes followed him back into the studio, where he began conversing with Alan.

Philip attempted to lip-read what was being said, then gave up. He focused his eyes on the grainy footage, and heard a faint whistling sound inside his ears. Perhaps it was only a latent result of the blasting feedback, or mild technical interference, but gradually it grew louder and more insistent. He was unsure whether it was coming through the enclosing basement walls, or from inside his own head.

'Take one,' Alan announced.

The whistling increased dramatically as the clip re-played. Philip, distracted by the incessant noise, attempted something vaguely satirical from the perspective of the helicopter pilot. He stalled temporarily as his eye caught sight of a man being decapitated. A roar of laughter emerged from the next room.

'Very good. Very, very funny.' The voice was Crew's. 'Again.'

Philip watched the figures rolling into far-off balls of

agony, obliterated by white lights of blazing gunfire; he could almost smell burning chemicals as the final victim cowered inside the cave entrance, awaiting the final streak of missile fire that would collapse a wall of overhanging rocks. The whistling noise sharpened as Philip adopted a voice he frequently used to amuse Mary. The jokes, disappointingly, he found himself stealing from an old Bill Hicks routine.

Crew appeared at the door. 'That's the one,' he said, beaming. 'I knew you had it in you.'

Alan handed back the phone.

'Sorry, can't fix that kind of thing.'

Philip, mortified, could scarcely believe what Crew had just done.

'And if Alan can't fix it, you're stuck.'

'I didn't put it there.'

'No?' said Alan. 'Then probably someone you know did.'

Crew gave a warning glance.

'See you at four. And don't be late, please.' The producer opened the stairway door for his departing client.

'Sure,' Philip said.

'For Mary, I mean.'

Philip climbed upwards, sensing more than mere sarcasm behind him.

'By the way, we'll be watching some pretty rare footage here tonight, if you're interested.'

He turned to find both men standing at the open door, watching him. They smiled oddly.

'With friends, of course,' added Crew. 'One of whom could probably solve that little problem of yours. If you really want the thing removed, that is.'

'Thanks,' said Philip. 'I'll bear it in mind.' He had almost made his way up into daylight when Crew spoke again.

'Remember to keep a receipt. Tell Mary I'm buying her dinner after all.'

He should have caught the tube. The train stood motionless before him in the sweltering midday heat, doors closed. Philip was waiting alone at the far end of the platform when he was blinded by a bright flash. Covering his eyes, he scoured the station, failing to discover who among the waiting passengers was shining the light deliberately into his eyes. The train doors opened without warning and the crowd moved forward, obstructing his view.

Philip's carriage, as he'd hoped, remained empty. The train moved off swiftly, passing beneath a series of small bridges, as he braced himself for the sudden black squeeze of the tunnel mouth leading toward Thameslink station. Soon he was trapped between its dark and gloomy walls, with occasional sights of sprawling subterranean passages marking his progress further underground, as the carriage speakers readied themselves for an announcement.

'Ladies and gentlemen,' uttered a rough metallic voice, 'We've been instructed to...'

The sound dropped out abruptly as the speakers failed, and Philip's ears were left to filter the train's violent mechanical rattlings as it careered even faster past the encroaching black brickwork of the tunnel.

Turning from the window in an attempt to forget how little space there was between himself and the walls, a small dot of light moving on the far door drew his attention. The tiny bright orb curved steadily from left to right upon the compartment window, swinging slowly like a pendulum tracing the shape of a smile upon the dark. It was the reflection of something moving in the carriage behind. Philip turned around but it had disappeared. Peering at the small glass window separating the two compartment doors, he could see nothing moving in the darkness beyond. Then a flash of electrical sparks thrown up from the rails below illuminated what was in there staring at him.

And smiling.

The train's brakes screeched their warning as Philip was catapulted into the seat opposite. The lights of his own carriage were extinguished in an instant, thrusting him into complete darkness. Meanwhile, something heavy, propelled by the swift deceleration of the train, made its way gradually toward him from the far end of the carriage, rolling purposefully beneath the seats toward his feet. Shocked by the force of the sudden stop, Philip tensed his muscles as a bulbous weight collided against the soft exposed soles of his shoes. He shifted his body upwards for leverage as his trainers slid on something wet. His right leg slipped back against the edge of a large, lumpish object. One side formed a small ridge against his foot and from it emerged a faint trickling sound, like released water, which slowed eventually to a steady drip.

Seizing the head rest in front of him with both hands, Philip kicked out with all his strength, grimacing as the heavy mass danced off weightlessly. Struggling to face his original position, he became aware of something round, barely visible, wafting itself lazily across the seat opposite toward the centre aisle. A faint breeze touched Philip as though a feather had been waved in front of his face.

He waited, terrified. Then it came again, stronger than before. The gentle brush of air skimmed his features, then retreated into the shadows. Philip began to entertain the unpleasant notion that someone was deliberately blowing into his face from close by. He inhaled a vaguely chemical scent as the soft gust reached him a third time, accompanied, he was convinced, by a faint whistling sound. Tentatively, he reached out toward it with his right hand.

It took a few moments to register the small wispy cord tracing lightly along the exposed edge of his knuckle, before an obscene hiss of escaped air discharged itself fully in his face, reeking of burnt rubber. He winced at the sounds piercing his ears, mechanical screams that intensified and wouldn't stop until two dim torchlights approaching from the carriage beyond somehow silenced the noise. By the time the train operators reached him, Philip had composed himself enough to accept their assurances that the train's mechanical failings would soon be set right. As they spoke, Philip refrained from glancing down at the glistening mess one of the torches had unwittingly exposed by his feet.

When the overhead lights returned there was nothing there, but as the train approached the crowded platform at Thameslink, Philip noticed a lone figure standing by the door, waiting to depart. Its front half was mostly hidden by a metal partition, but Philip had already glimpsed the silver-tinted raincoat standing motionless in the darkness of the far carriage. As he rose to identify his companion, the train doors slid open and the stranger stepped out. Bombarded by a crowd of irritable commuters barging forward, Philip managed to push past the worst of them onto the station floor. He saw the figure at the other end, approaching the stairs to the underground. Its coat blew wider than it had earlier that morning, and something now seemed to be moving beneath the folds, pushing and clawing against the thin material.

At times it looked, to Philip, like a face.

If it wasn't the evangelists preaching permanent sermons in Oxford Circus or Piccadilly, then the loudhailers Philip was hearing had to be a rally of some kind; and they were getting nearer. The sharp metallic voices and persistent drone of overhead surveillance helicopters did little to relieve his growing sense of helplessness. His anxiety swelled as he peered up at the huge business towers above. He stood beneath the tallest, where Mary worked and was at this second negotiating recently refurbished lifts that had rapidly acquired teething problems. Neighbouring blocks cast their black forms halfway down the building's side, smothering Mary's unseen descent in shadow. Philip shifted his eyes across to observe a small gleaming sphere ascend past the opposing structure. He watched it disappear behind a vast corner of concrete, then turned his attention instead to a confrontation taking place at the building's base; an altercation that looked increasingly capable of erupting into physical violence at any moment. Philip waited for it to start.

Mary's voice reached him long before he saw her, although she wasn't speaking to him. Beside her as she exited the entrance lobby strode an amiable-looking man in his mid-thirties, whom Mary introduced to Philip as David, and waved goodbye to moments later as Dave.

'Does he fancy you?' Philip asked when they finally took their seats in the small restaurant.

'I think so,' Mary replied, for once showing no trace of indecision in selecting her choice from the menu. Philip decided not to make his customary attempt at reconciliatory small talk, and Mary soon gave up waiting.

'So explain this,' she announced, presenting for his perusal her mobile phone. Upon it was frozen the now familiar image of a dead man's head.

'Crew sent it to you as well, then?' said Philip.

'You think it's *funny*?'

'Who said anything about it being funny?'

'You're smiling,' she snapped, forcing Philip to acknowledge the fact that he was. He suspected he might have been doing so for some time.

'It came through this morning,' Mary continued. 'It had *your* number and message, so don't treat me like an idiot. I've seen it already, anyway, on your computer.'

Mary gave the approaching waiter her order. A drink only. Philip decided against ordering food, and asked for a Coke.

'Crew sent it,' he explained. 'He thinks it's funny. He's the boss. No-one can sack him. I told him to stop.'

'Which he ignored.'

Philip nodded.

'But now you 'get' the joke.'

'He says my phone's picked up a virus.'

'Oh, please,' said Mary, turning to face the other diners. Picking up her mobile, Philip examined the grainy image trapped on its screen. Beneath ran a message he had no recollection of sending:

Mary, Mary, quite contrary, pretty heads all in a row.

A waiter opened a nearby window, and Philip heard once more the deep rasp of distant loudhailers. They were joined now by a great chorus of protesting voices bellowing slogans and chants; moving inexorably toward him. Police vehicles sped past as someone in the kitchen opposite switched on a television. The smooth, controlling voice behind the door revealed nothing of the words and images unfolding on screen, yet Philip caught vague impressions as harried waiters passed in and out; what he glimpsed mirrored what he heard in the streets outside.

Sirens converged simultaneously upon a nearby lane. Philip tore his attention from the window to catch Mary's chin rise up suddenly from its resting place on her hand. She can hear them too, he thought. She knows. But what precisely Mary did or did not know was unclear as her hand swept across her face to scratch idly at the taut plastic seam running along its right-hand side. Neither did she give any indication of the thoughts stirring within as her head twisted slowly round in his direction, dipping and bobbing uncontrollably, like a baby's, until it met the terrified gaze of his own face. Then, above smiling lips painted much too brightly, and clumsy simulated eyes seeking far too hard to distract him; beyond all the heavily and hastily applied make-up, Philip saw through to the crinkled, puffy lining of the rubber bag beneath.

He shut his eyes; kept them shut until he heard her pay the waiter who kept asking what was wrong with her 'husband'. The constant alarms covered the sound of Mary rising from her seat, drowning her parting words as she blew Philip the strange goodbye kiss that felt horribly familiar. He summoned enough courage to open his eyes and saw her in the street outside. At once he felt a desperate longing; an urge to protect her from what he knew was about to happen.

He ran to the restaurant door. She was at the tube entrance across the road now, her coat brushing against a police notice appealing for witnesses to a recent rush-hour murder.

Running after her, he fumbled change at the ticket machine, trying to ignore the armed police gathered behind each entrance barrier. He peered at her figure joining the escalator, then hurried through himself, racing down two steps at a time. At the bottom, she disappeared onto the southbound platform. He followed, attempting to block out overhead security warnings. Passengers were cramming themselves into packed carriages, an unlucky few rushing toward the far end in search of greater space. Mary was among them, squeezing into the train further down as Philip sprinted past the sound of closing doors. He threw himself into the carriage behind hers as doors slammed shut against him.

Shaking off his mounting claustrophobia, thankful at least that he was stood near an exit, he noticed several passengers staring moodily at his violent entrance. The reek of their bodies spread as Philip grabbed the overhead support rail and manoeuvred his head away from the open mouth of a large businessman. From here it was impossible to see through to the carriage beyond, and Philip needed some way of moving forward in order to locate Mary. As the tube pulled into the next station, he abandoned the notion of jumping off to board the next carriage. The platform was overrun and he dare not risk being shut out. Most likely Mary had a meeting with a client out of town; a thought that sobered Philip as he manoeuvred himself further forward and accidentally stepped on a woman's foot.

'Sorry,' he said, instantly.

'Funny, is it?' she snapped back.

Confused at the woman's response, and sweltering in the intense heat of the train, Philip trained his eyes on the blocked carriage end, hoping to spot Mary in the one beyond.

Someone coughed loudly in his face and Philip turned away in disgust, prompting an insult that he ignored, fearful of provoking further confrontation. He distracted himself by scrutinising a large bag lying on the floor beside him. When the train pulled out at Green Park, clearer than before, Philip realised it was still there, alone and unattended. He surveyed the other passengers, counting luggage for all but one, an Asian man who soon sensed hostile eyes upon him. Philip dropped his gaze instantly to a white badge displayed upon the man's jacket, which read 'I Quit Smoking. Ask Me How'. A woman left at Victoria, taking the unattended bag with her, and Philip felt ashamed. With more than a hostile glance, the reformed smoker also disembarked. Finally, Mary became visible in the centre of the neighbouring carriage.

Philip decided he would wait to see which station she was headed for and then follow. He wished to identify the person she was deep in conversation with; a figure hidden behind several other passengers, and whose hands made odd movements in the area below Mary's neck.

Their conversation grew more animated as the train moved on. Evidently Mary knew the person well, even if she hadn't yet noticed the tiny white fingers beneath her face, gripping and clutching at invisible string. Philip pulled down the ventilation window in front. At the same time, Mary disappeared from view as someone moved between them. Re-emerging seconds later, she was not alone. Inside a fat hood, bobbing about next to her with a frightful grin, was the stained black face of the silver balloon.

'Mary!' Philip shouted through the open window, alarming passengers behind and in front. She remained oblivious to his call, and to the silver head floating beside her, juddering with each heavy jolt of the train. It began to tap softly against her hair as the lights flickered, throwing her carriage into momentary darkness. It was enough to make Philip scream her name again through the open window, the filthy air blowing into his face, clogging his throat with dust.

'Mary!'

'Sit down!' shouted a voice from behind, which Philip ignored, terrified to discover that the balloon had now disappeared.

'Mary!' This time she heard him, and turned as a thick heavy arm grabbed Philip's and attempted to force him away from the window. He fought hard against it, prising off the fingers clasped over his eyes which now saw Mary's head twist about and smile, then crumple and bend at the centre as the top half drooped over awkwardly on one side. A thin whistle of escaping air filled his ears as Mary gradually caved in on herself, her face flopping backwards as its bottom half gave way uncontrollably. When her own right hand reached up to squeeze out what still remained inside, a flash of white brilliant light ensured Philip would see no more. He succumbed to the arms and bodies upon him, and to surrounding screams.

He emerged into daylight, eager to lose himself in the dispersing crowds. He'd managed to throw off his captors in the ensuing panic and make his way along the tunnel to an exit. Mary's voice had been close at times, and during those moments he had kept to the dark, letting others overtake him in their rush to escape what had at first felt like disaster.

Now, avoiding the suspicious glances of security officials and flustered underground staff, Philip looked across the road for an escape route. There was Mary, untouched and alive, laughing with others, comparing notes on shared experience. Between the smiles, however, Philip detected her anxious expression; observed how occasionally she parted from others to examine the faces of the crowd in search of someone else. Finally she found who she was looking for. She waved.

Philip stepped out into the road.

A huge collective intake of breath announced the coming impact. The body was struck head-on by the braking bus, rebounding hard off its shattered window with a sickening burst. Philip glimpsed the woman's face as she flew past him across the road, scraping along the rough tarmac in her silver-coloured raincoat before stopping several metres beyond the vehicle's front. The woman's pushchair, containing her child, lay on its side further up the road, smashed apart. A mylar balloon hung from the handle by a single string, unharmed. Its shadow sheltered the tiny wrecked body beneath from the burning sun.

Phil's reaction was different to others, he noted. A great many ran forward to stand around the bodies of the victims, uttering helpless words of reassurance. Others phoned simultaneously for ambulances, mixing confused details with absurd observations brought on by shock.

'Help them,' he heard Mary say, but he did not go with her. He was too busy recalling the woman's face; eyes screwed tight, mouth locked into a pained grimace as she twisted ludicrously through the air.

Music pounded from the shop front opposite as paramedics tried in vain to save lives. A man nearby hurled abuse at traffic wardens, angry at being directed past his right of way, unaware of what was being concealed from him.

Mary didn't cry, Phil observed, although others did. He himself did not. Instead he tried hard not to stare at the bodies, and the balloon, which none of the hands currently poised helplessly over the dead child had bothered to untie. It hung peacefully above everything, unscathed, smiling its black, oily smile. Their balloon, Phil realised, feeling suddenly calm. Not his, or Mary's, but theirs. As if to clarify something, the balloon lifted itself abruptly into the sky, its stained cord unravelling from the bloody chair handle. It floated upward, disappearing from sight into the limitless silence above.

Phil's mobile rang as Mary approached and put her arms around him.

'I knew her,' she said, stunned. 'I knew both of them.'

'Nightmare,' he replied, winking as he lifted the phone to his ear. 'Good afternoon, Alec. Guess what? I've just seen a road accident. Two. Nearly three. One was a kid. That's right, double points.'

Mary lifted her head toward his and pulled back from the cruel grin that greeted her.

'Awful sound,' Phil said, his eyes staring directly into hers. 'She popped just like a balloon.'

Mary retreated from the laughter, back toward the hidden darkness of the station entrance; to begin a search for something she knew was lost.

The Part of Me that Died

FRANK COTTRELL BOYCE

I went to school with Martin Hardy. You probably don't remember him but for about six months he was an answer in pub quizzes. He even made the 2007 edition of Trivial Pursuit. Martin was the actor who was sacked from the Teletubbies because his movements were supposedly 'too masculine'. The sacking got him coverage in broadsheet think-pieces as a martyr of 'political correctness gone mad' and, for a few weeks, he had his own male grooming slot on *Richard and Judy*. He came close to getting picked for *I'm a Celebrity Get Me Out of Here* but was pipped at the post by Timmy Mallett. I know this because he called me last week and told me all about it. This was a week before he was arrested for the apparent murder of his wife – Donna – who was found, smothered in her bed, yesterday.

No doubt tomorrow he will be back in all the papers.

I have known him a long time, but I don't know Martin well. I have seen him three times in the last ten years, including the last visit. All the same I was not surprised to hear that he had asked me to represent him. I'm sure he knows better solicitors. But none that have, as I have, a reason to believe in his innocence.

I did spend the evening of March 21st with Martin in his

flat in Salford Quays. We talked a good deal and we also watched some DVDs he had recently acquired of the children's television programme, *Rainbow*, featuring Zippy and George. He became quite agitated about these and insisted I watch them all – some three hours' worth – paying particular attention to Zippy's eyes. I left intending to inform his family about his mental state. But something prevented me. I felt in some way that I would be breaching a confidence. And – I hesitate to say so but feel that I must – I believe that perhaps he was not mad.

When I arrived at Salford West police station Inspector Williams gave me a copy of Martin's statement. I reproduce it here:

Statement of Martin Hardy

Donna was the love of my life and I wouldn't have hurt her for anything – ask anyone. From the minute we met – at the gala opening of the new flagship Miss Sixty clothes store in King Street, in 2008, we knew we had something in common and the moment we started talking this proved to be the case as we were both working for Andrew Morrow – the television producer – in similar fields.

We began to go out together and we have never looked back, even though we have had problems conceiving a child. We soldiered on together. You can ask the doctors.

Anyway a few weeks ago she started to act strange – staying out late and not explaining and that sort of thing. A lot of people might've thought she was having an affair or something but not her. And not me. And anyway, if she was, she would've tried to get it in the papers and I would know because we have the same agent. She looked drawn and tired. And I said to her, you have got to talk to me about this. Because we did talk about everything. But all she said was, 'You'll be next.' It was about this time that I started seeing someone hanging around the flat. When I was coming in after dark, or early in the morning. He was even there sometimes when I was out shopping and once I looked up and he was sitting opposite me on the night tram. If you find him, then you will get her killer. I can't describe him but others can.

I know that I am the 'others' referred to and I understand why Martin cannot offer a description himself so I am going to try. It's all I can do for him.

I wasn't close to Martin at school but he wasn't someone you were likely to forget either – charismatic, good-looking, good at sport. We all thought of him as the lad most likely to in our school. Of course when you're older, you realise that if your school is Bootle Beacon High, even the lad most likely to is not particularly likely to. In the great scheme of things.

I have one vivid memory of him, however, which has come to seem important. We were both in the 'gifted and talented' group at school and at the end of one summer term, we were taken – as 'motivational life experience' – to Granada Tours. I remember Martin kept staring longingly at all the doors marked 'Granada Personnel Only'. He was hungry for fame even then and he probably thought if he could just get through one of those doors, the people on the other side would somehow recognise him as one of their own, clasp him to their bosoms and anoint him with fame and cash.

Shortly after lunch he was watching a woman go in through one of these doors while talking on her mobile. The door did not snap to properly behind her. Without hesitating, Martin made straight for it, dragging me after him. We found ourselves in a long corridor, with doors leading off. I was extremely nervous and made the mistake of looking in the first door that stood ajar. Inside, a gruff, masculine voice was complaining loudly about something. We peeped in and saw something I have never forgotten – Matthew Corbett hurling Sooty across the room. Our eyes followed the puppet as it flew threw the air and we saw with horror that it landed in a bin full of damaged and discarded Sootys. There was no Sooty! Or at least, no particular and special Sooty. I know

now that it's a common folk belief in the Far East that a puppetmaker will have to find souls for each of his creations on the last day. I didn't know that then. Even so something in the depth of my being was revolted by the sight of the lifeless, damaged puppets. I looked at Martin and he too was staring vacantly at that basket of plush non-being. Even Corbett felt bad. Seeing us there, he shouted angrily and chased us away, slamming the door. Martin headed straight back to the exit. The heart had gone out of him.

I did not see Martin again until the Bootle Beacon Capital of Culture Reunion Barn Dance. He had by then acted for a few weeks in a soap opera, and appeared in an advertisement for Polar Iced Tea. I had just become a partner in a firm specialising mostly in accident compensation. It was natural we would end up together that evening. The man with the luminous blue nose from the iced tea advert and the junior partner in a firm of ambulance chasers – we were by far the most successful ex-students of our year. Martin listened politely while I talked about my wife – Ellie – and our daughter, Georgia. He even allowed me to show him some photographs before launching into a detailed chronology of his career.

To me, the advertisement for Polar Iced Tea – reasonably funny and seen by millions – seemed but a short step from Hollywood. He explained that a year had already passed since he'd shot it and in that time he had not received a single offer of work. He had however already met Andy Morrow who had already asked him to play the the masculine – alas, too masculine – Teletubby.

'Everyone says the Tubbies're going to be huge,' said Martin. 'I've been modelling for lunch boxes, posters, pencil sharpeners, you name it. I've even got a catchphrase, listen.' And he said, 'Biiiiig Hug' and hugged me.

'Very impressive,' I said.

'When I put that suit on,' said Martin, 'I feel like a part of me has died.'

The force, the vehemence, with which he said this, as much as the phrase itself, lodged in my mind. We exchanged cards. I never expected him to keep mine.

I was surprised when a few years later, he called my mobile and said he was 'just passing'. I wondered what he wanted. We live in Maghull. No one just passes Maghull.

He was well-groomed, thoughtful (he brought a bottle of wine), and entertaining. He played with Georgia until bedtime. I assumed he was thinking of starting a family and had come to see how someone of his own age and background liked it. When my wife went up to read Georgia her story, the two of us had a Laphroaig and he told me that he and Donna were indeed trying for a baby. They'd had certain problems and were 'trying everything'. They'd even tried 'doing it in their costumes'. Perhaps I haven't mentioned, during their first conversation, Donna and Martin had discovered that they had many things in common, including the fact that Donna too worked for Andrew Morrow. She was one of the Tweenies. The Tweenies belonged to Morrow too.

The vision of Tinky Winky making love to a Tweenie was one I found hard to deal with.

I probably withdrew into myself for a moment or two and when I started to listen to him again, his mood had darkened considerably. Nothing, apparently, had gone right since then. Morrow had sacked both him and Donna. They had still not conceived their baby. Richard and Judy had failed to ring. And it all started that day.

And something worse. Both he and Donna felt they had lost something. Something vital. Hard to describe what. But they had gone to IKEA together that day and bought nothing. Nothing in the whole shop attracted them. In the evening they had sat down to eat and could think of nothing that they wanted. This had gone on for weeks. This absence of want. 'That's why I've come here. You remember me. You knew me before. What did I like?'

I tried to think. 'I don't know, Mart. Same as the rest of us. A bit of a laugh. A game of footie. You were great in the school play, obviously. Wagon Wheels I seem to remember. You liked Wagon Wheels.' I did not remind him that the reason I knew this was that he was always taking mine.

'Wagon Wheels? Have you got any?'

I did have a few. I bought them to revel in the security of adulthood, in the fact that no one was going to take them. I showed them to him. He stared and shook his head. They did nothing for him now.

When Ellie came in and saw us with our whisky and Wagon Wheels she laughed. But even a sudden gust of self-consciousness couldn't lift Martin's mood. He stared at the Wagon Wheel like a man who has just taken a clock apart and put it together again and then found one cog wheel still lying on the carpet. Where does this bit go, he seemed to be thinking.

The atmosphere was so chilly that Ellie went to bed. I sat up a while longer while he rambled bitterly. He said, 'I remember thinking when I put on the costume, a bit of me died. Well what if it was this bit,' and he pointed to himself. 'What if I'm the bit that died? What if that's what this feeling is. Me and Donna. What if we're dead and the living bits of us are somewhere inside those costumes.'

I said, 'Thundercats.' He looked blank. 'You asked me what things you liked when you were at school. You were mad on Thundercats.'

But he was unreachable now. He started to talk about Morrow and how much he hated him. Apparently all the remaining Tubby and Tweeny actors had been sacked and replaced. 'And here's the thing, no one knows who the new ones are. Never hear a word about them down at casting. Never see them in the canteen. How d'you figure that then?'

'Well, I suppose he was pretty displeased at the negative attention he got from your sacking and is trying to be discreet this time, to protect his product.'

He must have thought I was being unsympathetic because he decided to leave then. I walked him to the door. As he walked away, he activated the security lights and I seemed to detect some sort of presence in his car. I shouted, 'Have you got a dog?'

'What?'

'Is that a dog in your car? You should've let it run round our garden.'

And he gave me a look of the purest astonishment, mixed with a kind of terror. He said nothing. But jumped in his car and drove away, almost in panic.

The next time I saw him was the 21st. I had just left the Law Courts and was walking up Deansgate and there he was. We exchanged pleasantries and I told him I was going to buy a new tie in Kendal's. He said that he was going to do the very same thing. We walked into the shop, passing first through the perfume department on our way to the lifts. There's a girl there I like to look at – just look at, that's all. She has bright, brass-coloured hair and very fair skin. It's a combination I like. I pretend to look past her while waiting for the lift. I noticed that Martin was doing the same thing. The girl noticed too and frowned, seeing this stereophonic gawping. In menswear, it was the same story. I would look at a tie. He would look at it straight after me. I would have assumed he was aping me, mocking me, if there had been any hint of pleasure in what he was doing. I remembered what he had said about being unable to find pleasure in anything, to want anything. And there was something dreadful, fearful in his behaviour, as though he was trying to remember how something was done.

He was like a puppet, each of whose strings was tied to one of my own nerve endings.

Out of pity I offered to buy him coffee in the café there. The waiter asked me what I wanted – I ordered a decaff cappuccino – Martin did the same. For conversation I said, 'United, eh?' And he said, 'United,' as though agreeing with me but then stopped and stared, waiting for some further prompt.

Embarrassingly when we had finished the coffee, he looked across the shop floor and bawled suddenly, 'Why are you all PRETENDING!?! Why!?'

I muttered something at him. And looked up. Hardly anyone had even glanced in his direction at the outcry. And, looking at the shoppers, it was possibly true. There was a terrible vacancy in their faces. Maybe Martin just had a more acute sense of this.

He told me he had sold his car and I ended up offering him a lift home. When I stopped to drop him off he was insistent that I come in with him. The flat was, at first glance, beautiful. At second, almost frightening. Looking at the Philippe Starck chairs and the Alessi kitchen accessories, I had the strongest sense that the people who lived there had taste but no preferences when it came to eating or even sitting. The whole thing had been copied from a magazine. It was an imitation of life.

He was in bad form that evening. I think I have mentioned this. He seemed to have reached some sort of crisis. He would not let me leave.

'I need to tell you,' he said. 'You're a solicitor. You'll be believed. And you have seen him.'

'Seen who?'

'I have a kind of presence.'

'You've always had that. That's exactly what the review said when you were in *Grease* in school. Martin Hardy has presence.'

'But now the presence is separate from me. It follows me. In a body of its own.'

'Like a stalker?'

'It's like he has come for me. It started weeks ago. At first it was from a distance. But just lately, he has got closer, much closer. A presence. Wherever I go, I know he is there. Sometimes I can see him plainly. The other night, on the tram. I looked up and he was sitting two seats ahead of me. He even turned his head towards me. I go out for a drink and he is on the other side of the bar.'

'Who?'

'Sometimes other people can see him. When I went swimming this morning, as I handed in my ticket the girl said, what about your mate? She could sense that I was shadowed. And you, you saw him plain. In the car, waiting for me. If you hadn't this would have been easier.'

'Why easier?'

'Because at first I thought I was going mad. I was grateful for that. I had felt so ... dead, that mental disturbance seemed encouraging, something to be enjoyed. And I noticed her too, Donna. She too would look behind her suddenly. Or look away suddenly from some empty space across the bar. I thought she was going crazy too. I thought it was nice. We would go mad together. Better than these months of endless blankness. I tried to talk to her about it. But she wouldn't talk. I know why now. I hadn't seen mine then. She'd seen hers. She was ahead of me.'

'Seen what?'

'I was at an audition. I got a call. I was sitting in reception reading the script. You know that they are watching you, looking at you, trying to form an impression of you without you knowing. I sat with my coffee, my script, my pencil. I was trying to look professional. I looked up. It was all I could do to stop myself crying out. He was standing behind the receptionist, making a hideous gesture at me.'

'Who?'

'This is it. This is the thing. I've read about, seen films about people haunted by children, by ghosts of parents, ghosts of children, by tortured souls. In the end, the haunted ones could speak about it. To someone. Gain help. Relief. But this... was ghastly. To be haunted like this. By something so hideously... comical. That no one would believe. No one would accept the horror of it.'

'Who was standing behind the receptionist? Who was on the tram?'

'Tinky Winky.'

To my credit, I did not laugh.

'He looked at me and mouthed the words, "Big Hug".'

I said, 'Well that was friendly, at least.' Perhaps I should've laughed. Perhaps he would've been relieved. He took my reaction as acceptance and moved up to another phase of higher madness. He whispered. 'But he's not a ghost. YOU saw him. You saw him waiting for me in the car.'

I said I couldn't be sure that it was Tinky Winky. I had thought it was a big dog.

'That was the first day I saw him clearly, that day at reception. Donna could tell right away that something had changed. We hugged each other. She'd been haunted by Milo. She had seen hers weeks ago. He'd got bolder. Other people had seen him. He'd even talked to them. Outside a branch of McDonald's, he'd even done a little dance. He never left her sight. He was like a child seeking attention. She knew he wanted something but she did not know what. She said, You're next Mart. I told her it had already started. But the point is, if other people can see them, these are not ghosts. These are not madness. These are real. It's not me who's mad, is it? It's Doc Morrow. He made them.'

'Made them?'

'I've been inside that suit. No human actor could stay

alive inside there more than an hour or so. It was hellish. These aren't actors.' He lowered his voice again, 'They're real. Don't you see? When he took our suits back, he had our genetic material. He has *engineered* something, creatures made of me and Donna. He has taken something from us and given it to them. The merchandising is alive. And we are dead.'

This is when he made me watch his *Rainbow* DVDs. We watched them frame by frame sometimes. Until he found the bit in an episode about kites where he claimed he could see real tears in Zippy's eyes. By then I thought I had listened enough. I left.

I feel of course that I should have contacted his family. I do occasionally see his father if I go to Mass in the cathedral. I could have alerted them but I didn't. So I feel some measure of responsibility for the dreadful events that followed. I was glad to be able to go to the police station and be briefed by him. I went through his rights with him and so on. He was polite, almost at ease. When I had finished the business in hand he said, 'Thanks for believing me.'

'You haven't asked me to believe anything. You haven't told me your version of what happened.' We really had only talked about his rights and so on.

'She ended up waiting in for him. I was there when he came. I saw it. Milo walked in through the door. She didn't try to avoid his gaze. She took his hand. She looked into his eyes and he smiled. That was the giveaway. Those things have fixed expressions but he smiled. She said, what d'you want, Milo? Quite tenderly and Milo said – it had a child's voice, and it could just about pronounce the word – it said, *Sister*. Then it hugged her. And hugged her and hugged her. Have you seen the way Micky Mouse hugs kids in Disneyland? It's a big hug. It was a big hug. Do you understand me? A biiiiiiig hug. And he didn't let go until she was lifeless, like those Sooty puppets we saw that day. Milo stayed for a while, stroking the body. Then it went.'

I thought for a while. 'Is that the story you want me to tell in court?'

He said, 'It won't come to that will it?'

He seemed so innocent, so blithe, at that moment that I couldn't bear to tell him the truth.

I realise now that I misunderstood this.

The next day, Martin was indeed in all the papers. Not just for the murder by suffocation of his wife. But for being the centre of a mystery of his own. A locked door mystery. He had been found suffocated too. On the floor of the high security holding cell in which he had been locked away all night. Several of his ribs had cracked under the strain of whatever it was that squeezed his last breath from him.

It was late October and all along Deansgate, the vivid faces of the toys and gifts stared out of the windows at the dull, panicky faces of the shoppers. They seemed to be watching each other, waiting for a signal from each other. And I thought again of what he had said: 'The merchandise is alive. We are dead.'

The Dogs

HANIF KUREISHI

Overnight it had been raining but to one side of the precipitous stone steps there was a rail to grip onto. With her free hand she took her son's wrist, dragging him back when he lost his footing. It was too perilous for her to pick him up, and at five years old he was too heavy to be carried far.

Branches heavy with sticky leaves trailed across the steps, sometimes blocking their way so they had to climb over or under them. The steps themselves twisted and turned and were worn and often broken. There were more of them than she'd expected. She had never been this way, but had been told it was the only path, and that the man would be waiting for her on the other side of the area.

When they reached the bottom of the steps, her son's mood improved, and he called 'chase me'. This was his favourite game and he set off quickly across the grass, which alarmed her, though she didn't want to scare him with her fears. She pursued him through the narrow wooded area ahead, losing him for a moment. She had to call out for him several times until at last she heard his reply.

Their feet kept sinking into the lush ground but a discernible track emerged. Soon they were in the open. It was a Common rather than a park and would take about forty minutes to cross: that was what she had been told.

Though it was a long way off, only a dot in the distance, she noticed the dog right away. Almost immediately the animal seemed bigger, a short-legged compact bullet. She knew all dogs were of different breeds: Dalmatians and Chihuahuas and so on, but she had never retained the names. As the dog neared her son she wondered if it wasn't chasing a ball hidden in the grass. But there was no ball that she could see, and the little speeding dog with its studded collar had appeared from nowhere, sprinting across the horizon like a shadow, before turning in their direction. There was no owner in sight; there were no other humans she could see.

The boy saw the dog and stopped, tracking it with curiosity and then with horror. What could his mother do but cry out and begin to run? The dog had already knocked her son down and began not so much to bite him as to eat him, furiously.

She was wearing heavy, loosely-laced shoes and was able to give the dog a wild blow in the side, enough to distract it, so that it looked bemused. She pulled the boy to her, but it was impossible for her to examine his wounds because she then had to hold him as high as she could while stumbling along, with the dog still beside her, barking, leaping and twisting in the air. She could not understand why she had no fascination for the dog.

She began to shout, to scream, panicking because she wouldn't be able to carry her son far. Tiring, she stopped and kicked out at the dog again, this time hitting him in the mouth, which made him lose hope.

Immediately a big long-haired dog was moving in the bushes further away, racing towards them. As it took off to attack the child she was aware, around her, of numerous other dogs, in various colours and sizes, streaming out of the undergrowth from all directions. Who had called them? Why were they there?

She lost her footing, she was pushed over and was huddled on the ground, trying to cover her son, as the animals noisily set upon her, in a ring. To get him they would have to tear through her but it wouldn't take long, there were so many of them, and they were hungry too.

Safe as Houses

CHRISTINE POULSON

'Can't you hear it?' She's shaking his shoulder.

'What? What?'

'The baby! There's a baby crying! Can't you hear it?' She speaks urgently.

The green light of the digital alarm clock says 4.10. Guy gropes for the light and switches it on. He squints at Mary.

She's sitting up in bed beside him. She looks blindly around. Her eyes are open, but she's not seeing him.

'Is it Toby?' he asks.

'Not Toby! The baby!'

He listens. The house is silent. He puts a hand on her arm.

'It's alright,' he says gently. 'You're dreaming. Go back to sleep.'

He speaks to her as if she were a child, and like an obedient child she lies down again. He smoothes her dark hair back from her forehead. She sighs and turns on her side. She slips a hand under her pillow, a childhood habit that he finds endearing even after all these years. He tucks the duvet round her and turns the light off. He lies on his back beside her, his heart still beating fast from the shock of being pulled out of deep sleep.

Her dream has disturbed him in more ways than one. He feels alert, restless. He gets out of bed. There is no need to pull on a dressing gown over his t-shirt and boxer shorts. The infra-red sensors will detect the increased movements and

35

adjust the heating automatically. He doesn't bother to switch on the lights either. Except in the bedrooms that face the road, they rarely draw the blinds. Most of the house looks out onto a garden surrounded by a tangle of trees and beyond that there's a golf course. Visitors find it hard to believe that a house can be half-an-hour's drive from the centre of London yet be so secluded.

Tonight there's a full moon, a hunter's moon, in a frosty November sky. A pallid light pours in through the huge glass wall that takes up one side of a sitting room that spans the entire length of the house. He trails his fingers along the back of the pale leather sofa, enjoys the feel of the polished wooden floor under his bare feet. People tend to think that minimalism doesn't go with family life, but they're so wrong. As long as you have plenty of storage space and can accept a bit of wear and tear, it's perfect. Kids love these big open spaces. Plenty of room for Toby to ride around on his tricycle when he's big enough for one, and that won't be long.

He pads into the kitchen and pours himself a glass of cold milk. He lingers by the control panel for the smart house system and runs his fingers over the wall-mounted touch screen. The sensors can pick up even the movements of a sleeping child and small red blips on a floor plan of the house register that he is in the kitchen and Mary and Toby are in bed upstairs. Absolutely state-of-the art, and so it should be. It's his business, after all, he designs smart house systems, and if he can't have the best, who can?

On the way back to bed, he takes a detour. Toby's room and the nursery are in what is almost a separate little annexe with its own bathroom and a spiral staircase that leads down to the sitting room. He looks in on Toby. The bedside lamp is designed so that the heat from the bulb makes the shade rotate; Elmer the patchwork elephant and his friends chase one another endlessly, hypnotically, around the ceiling. Toby is lying on his back, his arms flung out, fingers gently curling. Guy leans over the bed and puts his hand on his blonde, thistledown hair. Toby doesn't stir. He's almost two, and still not talking much. The doctor thinks it's nothing to worry about. Guy hesitates on the landing and then opens the door to the nursery. He doesn't go in but stands in the doorway, taking in the cot, the sheepskin rug, the mobile, all clearly visible in the moonlight. But it's the changing mat on the chest of drawers that tugs at his heart. It has an air of innocent readiness, as if it doesn't know what has happened to the baby. The miscarriage was a late one – twenty weeks – and Mary lost a lot of blood. It was only a few months ago and she is still grieving. That is surely what her dream was about.

Back in bed, he presses himself against Mary's back, slips his arm around her waist. He inhales the fresh scent of her hair, matches his breathing to hers, and is soon asleep.

In the bustle of the following morning he doesn't mention the dream, and neither does Mary. She works three days a week as an editor for a small independent publisher and it's one of her days in the office. Guy is going away for a couple of days to design a system for a care home in Cumbria and their talk is all of practicalities, when to put out the rubbish, who's going to pick up the shopping. A quick kiss and a ruffle of Toby's hair and Guy's gone. He gets home late on the Thursday. Mary's already asleep. He undresses in the bathroom and without turning on the light, slips into bed beside her. He's asleep in moments —

A thin, high wail, visceral, tugging at his guts. He's sitting up before he even knows he's awake. He puts out a hand, but Mary's not there. He gets out of bed and goes out onto the landing. The crying has stopped – no, it begins again. And then he realises – it's not a baby, it's his wife. The door to the nursery is ajar. He pushes it open and switches on the light. Mary is running her hands over the wall next to the chest of drawers. She turns to him.

'Where is it? Where it is?' Her face is glossy with tears.

'What? Where's what?' His voice sounds shrill and panicky.

'The door! I can't find it.' She grabs his arm, gripping so tightly that he winces.

Her desperation is infectious. He finds himself looking at the wall as though there might be a door that he has forgotten about.

'Mary,' he says gently, 'There's no door. It's a blank wall.'

'It's always the same,' she says later, sipping the hot chocolate Guy has made her. He's lying beside her propped up on one elbow, watching her face.

'It's happened before?' he says.

She nods. 'It's only on nights when you've been away that I've actually got out of bed.'

'Until tonight.'

'Until tonight. I dream I'm woken up by a baby crying. I go into the nursery and I'm surprised when I see an empty cot in the moonlight. I'm expecting to see her there. I start to panic. I go around the house, bumping into things in the dark and looking for her in the most unlikely places, in cupboards, even inside the washing machine one time. She's still crying and I'm desperate. And then I realise. Yes! There's a room I haven't searched. The secret room. I must have put her there to keep her safe. I'm so relieved. But only for a moment. Because the secret room isn't always in the same place. Where is it tonight? I start running my hand along the walls to find the door knob or the hinge of the door. And all the time, the baby's crying, I can't bear it. And then I find it, the doorknob, and that's usually when I wake up. Before I can open the door. But once —'

Her hands are clasped round the mug. She's gazing into the distance.

'But once —' he prompts.

'It was so real. I could feel the door knob, smooth and round in my palm, one of those old-fashioned wooden ones. I pulled at it – a door started to open in the wall, I could see a brilliant light – the baby had stopped crying, she knew I was coming, and then —'

'And then?'

'Toby shouted for me and I woke up. He must have had a bad dream. It took me ages to calm him down. He came into bed with me in the end.'

Tears are welling up her eyes.

'Oh darling.' He pulls himself up beside her and puts an arm round her.

'It's all so real. I can't tell you. Not like a dream. And when I wake up, I'm in the nursery.'

'You must have been sleep-walking.'

'Oh, Guy, you don't think she could be – I don't know, could she be somewhere – and wanting me?'

'Hey,' he says, more sharply than he intends. He turns to her, takes the mug and puts it on the bedside table. He holds both her shoulders and looks into her face.

He says, 'You know what the doctors said, she wasn't viable. It was too soon.' He hesitates, wondering how to go on. Should he remind her that they are both atheists, they don't believe in souls or an afterlife, there's only here and now, this material world —

He doesn't have to decide, because something happens that makes the hairs stand up on his arms.

Somewhere in the house a baby is crying.

This time Mary isn't dreaming – unless he is, too.

The following week Guy does a detour on the way back from visiting a private client in Shropshire and meets Jessica in a café in Birmingham near the library where she works.

Jessica is Mary's twin. They're not identical, but there's a resemblance that Guy finds unsettling. Truth to tell, he's always fancied her a bit – something to do with forbidden fruit – and he wonders if she feels the same way. Not that either of them would ever do anything about it.

'I realised what it must be,' Guy tells Jessica. 'The baby monitor was on. It was picking up signals from outside the house, probably that block of flats just down the road.' He taps the ash off his cigarette.

'Who switched the monitor on?' Jessica asks.

'We think it must have been Toby. He loves switching things on and off. I could've just changed the frequency, and then I thought what the hell – I disabled it completely so that he can't switch it on again.'

'But could he reach?'

'He's got one of those plastic step-up things. You know, like a stool. He uses it to get things out of the fridge.' He takes a deep drag and exhales the smoke through his nose.

'I thought you'd stopped smoking?'

'I have. Don't tell Mary.' He grinds out the cigarette, giving it one last vicious twist in the ashtray.

'So just a glitch in the machine?'

'Oh God yes, what else could it be?'

'That's the question, isn't it? You know, Mary wanted that baby so badly. Perhaps she's making it happen somehow.'

'Oh please!'

'I'm serious. Poltergeists have been well documented. They're connected with psychic disturbance.'

'I thought they were usually associated with adolescents.'

'So you do know about it?'

'Yeah – I've heard of it, but, Jess, I can't believe we're having this conversation. It's a technical problem, that's all, but it's had a really bad effect on Mary. She's been dreaming about the baby.'

Jessica nods. 'She told me on the phone.'

'Did she tell you she's been sleep-walking too?'

She frowns at him over her latte. 'No, she didn't.'

He reaches out for his cigarettes, but Jessica puts her hand on them. He grimaces. 'You're right. It won't help.'

They are both silent for a few moments.

Jessica says, 'Mary needs to get pregnant again.'

'I know, but at this rate...' He gives an eloquent shrug. 'Neither of us are sleeping properly, and Toby's started getting into bed with us at night. He knows something's wrong, poor little devil. I'm dreading Christmas. If the baby had gone to term, it would have been her first one... '

'Yeah, Mary's bound to be thinking about that. Look, why don't I come and stay over Christmas?'

'I was so hoping that you'd say that. I suggested it to Mary, but she put me off – I mean, you always do your charity stuff?'

'They'll have to manage without me for once.'

'You'd better let her think it was all your idea. And by the way, I didn't tell her I was meeting you.'

'It *was* my idea, wasn't it? I'll ring Mary tonight.'

Guy feels that Jessica's presence will change the dynamics of the situation. If she hadn't offered to come, he'd intended to ask her. As he drives home in the rain he congratulates himself on the way that he's handled the situation and wonders if Mary will guess that he had a hand in Jessica's decision.

It's dark when he turns into his street and it's made darker by the dripping trees that filter the light from the street lamps. As he slows down to turn into their drive the headlights pick up a small figure walking along the pavement. He can hardly believe his eyes. It's Toby. Guy stops and gets out of the car. Toby's face crumples. He sees from the look on Guy's face that he shouldn't be out here on his own.

Guy squats down in front of him and speaks gently. 'What are you doing out here, little man?'

'See Dada.'

'You wanted to see me come home in the car?'

Toby nods enthusiastically.

'Let's go in out of the cold, shall we?'

He picks Toby up, his anger mounting. How could Mary have let this happen? The road isn't very busy, but how busy does it have to be for a toddler with zero road sense? As if to make the point, a car approaches, picking up speed as it passes them. Is Mary so preoccupied with the child they didn't have that she can't look after the one they've got?

The side door is open, the tell-tale plastic stool just inside the threshold.

He goes through into the kitchen.

Mary is at the far end, chopping something up. He notes almost with detachment that her hands are bloody. She looks up and smiles, but when she sees his expression, the smile freezes on her face.

'Toby was outside. On the pavement.'

She shakes her head. 'No, no.'

'I tell you he was. How the hell did he get out of the house?'

Her eyes turn to the monitor attached to the wall less than a metre away. She looks back at Guy then back to the monitor, pointing at it with her knife. She's shaking her head again. He doesn't understand, until he sees what she is seeing: a pulsing red blip on the screen.

According to the smart house system there is someone upstairs in Toby's room.

The next moment the blip is gone, but they've both seen it. Guy puts Toby down and goes upstairs. Of course there's no-one there. He comes back to the kitchen, opens a bottle of red wine and pours two large glasses. He gulps his down in seconds and pours a second one. Mary is sitting with Toby on her lap, and he is curled up against her, thumb in mouth. Guy and Mary exchange glances. She says, 'I'm sure

I didn't leave the door open.' There isn't much to be said. They both know there is something seriously amiss.

'After supper I'll strip the system down and test every link,' he says.

He turns to the chopping board to take up the cooking where Mary left off. Strips of lamb's liver are laid out in a neat row and there's a cabbage waiting to be shredded. Liver and leafy green vegetables, recommended by the doctor to remedy a slight anaemia before Mary tries again for a baby. He feels a flicker of hope for the future.

They may live in a minimalist house, but that doesn't mean they have to have a minimalist Christmas. They stick mostly to white, and silver, and gold, and Mary goes to town on the tree. This year it's so big that the star on the top only just clears the ceiling.

Guy pours himself another small glass of vodka and settles back on the sofa. He relishes this little island of calm in a busy day. It's ten o'clock on Christmas Eve and they've only just managed to get Toby to go to bed. Mary and Jessica are upstairs with him now. Guy is looking forward to seeing his face in the morning. His tricycle, wrapped in Thomas the Tank Engine paper, is hidden in the garage.

Mary keeps up a tradition, instigated by her Polish father – both parents have been dead for some years – of celebrating Christmas Eve with a special Polish meal. Mary and Jessica spent hours this afternoon in the kitchen making blinis and bortsch, while he took Toby out to the park. This is the time of year he misses his own parents who live now in New Zealand with his sister and her family. Out in the garden white fairy lights are strung in the trees and for the last few hours snow has been gently falling. The reflection of the room is superimposed on the wintery garden, giving him the disconcerting feeling that there is another room out there even whiter and more elegant than the one he's sitting in. And he feels a mild frisson when the door in the reflection opens. Jessica comes in. He looks back into the real room and raises his glass to her.

She gives him a smile and a wink.

'Mary's tired. She's decided to go to bed. Why don't you go up, too?'

'The clearing up —'

'I'll do it.'

He has a last check before he goes up. There've been no problems since he replaced the infra-red sensor in Toby's room. He still can't work out how the back door came to be unlocked and he is inclined to think that was Mary's fault, though for the sake of marital harmony he hasn't said so. He overhauled the system just to be on safe side, paying particular attention to the sensors in the nursery. He has a feeling that it might not be all that long until they need them again. And that feeling increases when he sees that Mary is wearing her favourite nightdress — a long, white cotton affair — and catches a whiff of Diorissimo as he climbs in beside her. She's propped up on the pillows reading Vogue. He leans over and presses his lips to her neck just below her ear. She lets the magazine fall to the floor.

He kisses her mouth and, wrapped in an embrace, they slide down between the sheets. He hopes she hasn't put in her diaphragm.

'Mummy!'

Mary's body tenses. Guy groans. Over her shoulder, he sees Toby at the bedroom door.

'What's the matter?' he asks. But Toby can't say. He only knows that he is upset and wants to get into bed with mummy and daddy.

'Guy?' says Mary.

Guy heaves a sigh. 'Oh, alright, let him come in for a bit.'

He sticks out an arm and hauls the child in. Toby clambers over him and squirms in between them.

Guy decides to give it ten minutes. Then he'll take Toby back to his own bed.

Five minutes later they are all fast asleep.

He's trekking over bleak moorland. It's cold, so cold, and somewhere ahead of him are Mary and Toby. He's afraid that he'll never catch them up. He thinks he hears something. Is it the cry of a baby? It's hard to be sure above the whistling of the wind. He stands and listens, strains to catch the sound. And then in that strange way that the mind works, he is aware that he is dreaming and struggles to wake up.

He's lying in bed with Mary asleep beside him. Did something wake him? The house is silent, but it's a silence that feels like the aftermath of a sound. It's as though the reverberations haven't quite died away. He props himself up, listens intently. There's nothing. But still he is uneasy. The room isn't as dark as usual. The door is open a crack and there's a light on somewhere in the house.

He gets out of bed and goes out onto the landing. The light is coming from the kitchen. When he opens the door, blinking in the light, he feels a slight shock because it looks as if Mary is sitting at the kitchen table. Of course it's Jessica. She's wearing a long white dressing gown that reminds him of Mary's nightdress. Startled, she looks round and her face relaxes when she sees that it's him.

'Couldn't sleep?' he asks.

She shakes her head. 'And you?'

'A bad dream.' He realises that he was probably woken up by Jessica coming down the stairs.

He glances at the clock on the cooker. 4.20. He rubs his chin, feeling the stubble rough under his fingers. He's dressed only in boxer shorts and a t-shirt. He feels a little self-conscious.

'Fancy a cup of tea?' he asks.

'Go on then.'

He puts the kettle on and yawns. Jessica yawns with him, and they laugh.

He pulls out the chair opposite Jessica and sits down. Jessica's face is shiny and her hair untidy. There's something special about being awake with someone when the rest of the world is asleep. He remembers when Toby was a baby and he used sometimes to wake up when Mary was giving him his night feed, how cosy and intimate it was.

'Have you done Toby's stocking?' Jessica asks.

'Good question. No, I haven't.' He remembers now that Toby was in bed with him. Mary must have woken up and taken him back to his own room.

He gets up and goes to the smart house monitor, runs his fingers over the keypad. A plan of the first floor unfolds and two red blips show both Mary and Toby asleep in their respective beds.

Jessica pulls the lapels of her dressing gown together and rubs her arms. 'It's a bit cold in here.'

He checks the temperature. It's 60 degrees, should be fine, but she's right. There's a positive chill in the air.

The kettle clicks off. But Guy doesn't move towards it. It's getting colder and now there's a draft coming from somewhere. It's as though a window is open somewhere in the house. There's a faint sound, like a distant banging, as if a latch has broken, allowing a door to swing back and forth.

'The wind –' Jessica says and breaks off, her mouth half open, her head tilted to one side. Then he hears what she's hearing,

'It sounds like a baby,' she says. 'There's a baby crying. The monitor –'

'Impossible. It's not wired up.'

The crying has become a gasping staccato wailing. There's a strange quality to it, a kind of echo as if it's been amplified.

Jessica is on her feet, her hand is at her throat and her face is white. 'What's going on?'

He turns to the screen which still shows Mary and Toby

on the first floor. He flips over to the ground-floor plan.

'There's nothing here – just us.'

He flips back to the first floor map and this time something has changed. The red blip that is Mary is no longer in bed. It's moving across the bedroom and has reached the door.

Propelled by an urgency he doesn't understand Guy turns away from the screen and pushes open the door into the hall. He is hit by a blast of icy air. He slaps his hand down on a bank of switches. Instantly the hall and stairway are flooded with light.

Mary is on the landing moving in the direction of Toby's room and the nursery. The crying is getting louder, the air pulsates with the relentless, despairing wail. The draft has become a wind – pushing back her hair and moulding her nightdress to her body. As Guy plunges up the stairs he feels its force, pressing against him, carrying with it a smell of something dank and decaying. He's after Mary like a dog chasing a hare and she must have moved like a hare, because when he reaches the top of the stairs she's gone. Is that the skirt of her nightdress flicking out behind her as she disappears into the nursery?

How long does it take Guy to follow her into that dark room? A second? Two seconds? For a moment, he thinks he's got her, that her nightdress is in his grasp, but no, it slips through his fingers. He flicks on the light. The homely scene springs into the light: the cot, the changing mat, the sheepskin rug. The crying stops as abruptly as if it's been switched off. Mary's not there. The empty room stares blandly back at him.

He backs out and opens Toby's door. The little boy is sitting up in bed, his eyes wide. Guy sees that he is too frightened even to cry. When he picks Toby up there's something reassuring about the solid little body and the way that Toby clings to him. Now that the crying has stopped, Guy's panic is subsiding. He must have imagined that he saw

Mary going into the nursery. She'll have gone down the spiral stair to the sitting room. She's probably in the kitchen with Jess.

But when he goes down with Toby in his arms, there's only Jess, standing by the smart house monitor.

'Where's Mary –'

'She went out.'

'She went out!' Guy can't believe what he's hearing. 'In her nightdress?'

Jessica nods. 'I saw her.' She touches the screen. 'This door up here. But you must have seen her. You were right behind her when she went into the nursery.'

He shakes his head. 'There isn't a door in that wall. There isn't even a window.'

She's staring in confusion at the screen. 'No, of course there isn't. But I was sure...'

He moves to her side. According to the floor plans there is no-one on the first floor. On the ground floor there is only Jessica, Guy and Toby.

Guy goes round the house and checks that the doors and windows are all locked from the inside. He switches on all the lights so that the house is ablaze like an ocean liner. In silence Jessica and Guy search the house from top of bottom, opening cupboards and looking under beds. When they've finished, they do it all over again. After that they go into the nursery. It's as if they are waiting for something. The house is warm now. Toby is asleep on Jessica's shoulder. Guy thinks there's a trace of Mary's perfume in the air. As he gazes out of the window, he sees below him an unblemished carpet of snow, bluish-white in the light of the moon.

They stand there for a long time, until at last the late grey dawn of Christmas Day steals over the garden.

By common accord, without speaking, they turn away and go down to the kitchen, to decide what they are going to tell the police.

The Coué

JEREMY DYSON

Charlie Thoroughgood had heard the word 'Coué' before. He even knew what it meant. But he never expected to see the dreadful thing.

His premises occupied a small shop on a large concrete housing estate to the north of Sheffield. Saffron Lane as it was known – though there was no lane, and nothing as delicate as saffron in evidence – was one of a number of council estates built in the post-war period that was now due for demolition. Many of the residents had fled, rehoused in brighter, more anonymous accommodation. None mourned their move but Charlie himself felt a strange affection for the place. It was true he didn't have to live there – he could drive straight into a garage at the rear of the shop and let himself in – but there was something about the cheerless slabs and weed-cracked paving that spoke to him, and the more deserted it became the more he took to wandering the walkways and paths come lunchtime. He didn't care to be there after dark, but that was just expediency. Besides, Janet wouldn't let him.

He'd never relied much on passing trade – obviously, since this location could hardly be expected to generate it. There were few other retailers in the vicinity, apart from an off-licence and a charity shop. But even in the days before the internet his business – 'Ubu Suku' – had built up a healthy mail-order client base. The subtitle on his stationery read 'World Curios'. Charlie thought it made his venture sound trite but it worked as a description and it kept the orders coming so he had resisted the temptation to alter it for the website. Besides, Janet wouldn't let him.

And there was nothing trite about Charlie's expertise. His customers knew that. His depth of knowledge, his breadth of stock – his contacts and trading partners were unparalleled.

The shop itself was effectively a warehouse and an office, but he liked the fiction that it was a premises for customers. He took great delight in arranging the displays, the theatre of it, making it seem as if the place was from another time – some magical Victorian emporium on Great Russell Street or in Mayfair. That was an era when collecting and classifying was seen as a noble pursuit, a branch of academia. A time when much of the world was still veiled in mystery and men such as Charlie were seen as entrepreneurs, purveyors of enlightenment and knowledge. Though current regulations and fashionable opinion threatened to make Charlie a pariah he persisted in his trade with a passion and bullishness his Victorian forbears would have been proud of.

When Charlie raised the electric security shutters this particular morning, he was surprised to see a figure through the painted glass of the front door. Charlie slid the bolts carefully, then pulled the door towards him. The man, for it was a man, almost fell inside. He had been facing the other way, studying the concrete desolation of the dilapidated concourse. He turned and grinned foolishly, revealing a set of prominent teeth. They were arranged in an unusually sharp curve, suggesting a physiognomy more rodent than human. He looked academic and gentrified, so it was a surprise to hear a heavy Essex accent when he spoke.

'Mr Thoroughgood?'

'Yes,' said Charlie.

'Mr Charles Thoroughgood?' The 'Charles' emphasised as if there might be a hundred Thoroughgood's on the premises, but only one of any fame and distinction.

'Yes,' said Charlie again, determined to offer no more. The man held out his hand. It was narrow and girlish, but the skin was rough and calloused, and the fingertips stained and sore-looking. Charlie gave it a perfunctory shake.

'Collins. Rudolph Collins. It's an honour sir. A pleasure and an honour.' The man bustled inside the shop. He carried several bags – mostly of the battered looking polythene variety, though there was one large canvas item – like an old-fashioned camper's. 'It took a little initiative to get here,' he said, laying the bags down at his feet. 'A map of the local bus services took me so far, but I'm afraid I made several wrong turns.' He looked up at Charlie. 'Still,' he said, suddenly smiling. 'I'm here now.' Charlie tried to busy himself around the shop, moving behind the main counter, withdrawing a pile of invoices from beneath a paperweight. But Mr Collins, moved towards him. He picked up the paperweight, cupping it in his hand. It was a block of crystal containing a large black spider. 'Haplopelma minax,' he said. 'Female. Very nasty.' Again the big grin revealing the inhuman teeth.

'And how can I help Mr..?' said Charlie, trying not to sound in any way friendly. He was suspicious of the man and hoped that he would leave. He would be quite happy to turn away the custom.

'Collins. Rudolph Collins,' said the man again. He put the paperweight down and stepped forward, his own face stopping just short of Charlie's. His breath smelt of peppermints, and something worse beneath. 'If I were to say the word 'Coué' to you,' said the man, 'what would you think?'

'I'm sorry,' Charlie said.

'Come come, Mr Thoroughgood. You know what a

Coué is. I'm sure of that.' He smiled again. Charlie thought about the man's skull, what it would look like stripped of skin and cartilage. Not quite human.

'I couldn't get you one. It's against the law to trade such an item.' No need to play games with the man. Charlie smelt entrapment. Let's speed through this charade, he thought, and get him off the premises.

'So you do know what I'm talking about.' The man raised his eyebrows. His eyes were bright and alive with excitement.

'There's nothing more to discuss,' said Charlie. He turned away from the man, standing upright. He picked up the pile of invoices. Mr Collins stayed where he was, studying Charlie as he moved away from behind the desk.

'Oh I know you couldn't get me one. I wouldn't expect to come here and have you get me one. One doesn't wander into a shop – even a shop such as this – and say, excuse me I would like a Coué please. In fact I'll take two, if you have them.'

'To tell you the truth Mr…Collins, I doubt that such a thing actually exists.'

'Indeed. Yes. I doubted that the Hand of Glory actually existed. Until I located one in the private collection of a Mr Ammar from Whitby. It sits now, as we speak, on the mantelpiece in my study. I don't ever light it of course. I might fall asleep and never wake up.' Charlie wasn't going to respond to such a lure. He moved towards the office area, beneath the shelf of puffer fish. 'But the Coué…' the man had no intention of shutting up. 'The Coué does exist. You see I have one with me. Here. In this bag. I was wondering if you might like to buy it.' He grinned, like a conjurer having pulled something delightful from an empty box.

'What?'

'Come come, Mr Thoroughgood. I'm offering you a once in a lifetime opportunity.' There was something fervent about his entreaty. Something desperate.

'I'm a businessman. What good is there in stock I can't sell on.'

'Mr Thoroughgood – '

'Thank you. I've a very busy morning ahead.'

'Mr –'

'Thank you.'

Later, after the man had left Charlie went into his office and sat looking at the photo of Janet above the computer. She was thinner then – good looking. Less flesh on her face. He could just imagine what she might have to say were he to spend a thousand pounds on such an item. Not that he would have done so. He had refused even to look at it.

'This came for you.' It was the first thing she said to him when he got home. Janet was holding an envelope. It was grubby and brown, like it had been forgotten at the bottom of a bag for a year or so.

'What do you mean 'came for me'?'

'You're in a good mood. Charming.' She came over and pressed her lips wetly against his cheek, giving him a half-comical kiss. He took the envelope, watching her walk across the room. Her big arse. The idea of touching it momentarily repulsed him. 'I've been speaking to your mother,' she said.

'What?'

'About child care.' Charlie didn't respond. He examined the envelope. The slanting handwriting written with a fountain pen. 'She thinks she could manage two days.'

'And the other three?' he said. 'It's thousands. In a year. If we pay for it. It adds up you know.'

'Charlie. We'll find a way. Everybody manages.' Charlie looked inside the envelope. A lone business card, tatty and dog-eared. Rudolph Collins. A mobile number written on the back. 'Call me.'

Later, sitting in his room. His private room, surrounded by his personal collection. It was where he felt safest. Among his things. The ivory puzzle balls. The lizard skeletons. The scarab beetles and scorpions. The two headed calf that had been on display at Ripley's Believe it or Not on Hollywood Boulevard. He reached for a book from the shelf above the display cabinets. Lewis Spence's *Encyclopaedia of Occultism*. It was a long time since he'd examined it. It had been a favourite of his childhood. He remembered a long summer's day. Nine years old. Cricket at school in the afternoon. It seemed strange now, his childhood interest in something so esoteric. It had felt so normal at the time. He leafed through the pages. There was a woodcut of the Hand of Glory. Like the one that supposedly resided on Rudolph Collins mantelpiece. He had wanted nothing more than to see such a thing as a child. The idea of owning one would have been quite unbelievable. He flicked further on. A blade of long grass caught in the junction of paper and binding. The entry for the Coué. An engraving of the hideous curled-up thing. 'The Coué is mummified body of baby – a girl–child of less than six months bred and then slaughtered...' A rhythmic knock.

'Chuck?' The door opened. Janet's face, plump and round filling the crack. She edged her way within tentatively, as if to emphasise her own sensitivity. 'Do you want an Options?' She held out a steaming mug – a sickly butterscotch smell rising from it. Charlie shut the book. 'Maybe I'll work part-time. If I go freelance. I could earn more money on three days than I do on five.'

Charlie tapped the computer keyboard making the screen spring into life, hoping that she wouldn't notice it had been in sleep mode. He nodded. 'Maybe. Let's think about it. Do some sums.'

'Charlie.' He sipped at the hot chocolate. Tasted powder. He could hear the waver in her voice. Knew that if

she sensed his ambivalence she would be upset. He reached
out for her and squeezed her arm.

'No really,' he said. 'We will.'

She looked around at the collection. 'It's time you got
rid of all this. You know that don't you?' She pulled her arm
away from his and walked out.

'Mr Collins?' Charlie hadn't expected him to answer. 'Are
you still here?'

'Mr Thoroughgood. I can be with you this afternoon.
This afternoon.'

And Rudolph Collins was there that afternoon in the same
clothes as before, still carrying his polythene bags. Charlie
wouldn't have been surprised to find he'd been sleeping under
a bridge.

'I took the liberty of bringing my own cup of tea. I hope
you don't mind.' He held out a polystyrene cup. He pulled at
the cover. His hands were shaking. He looked sweaty and ill.
He sipped at the drink, drawing it through his ratty teeth.

'And have you got the... Are you still willing to sell – ?'

'Oh yes Mr Thoroughgood,' said Collins, looking over
his shoulder. 'I'm willing to sell. I'm ready and willing to sell.'
He hauled his canvas bag up on to the desk. Putting down his
tea he began to work at the buckles, fingers moving quickly and
eagerly, despite the tremens. He withdraw a large object
wrapped in newspaper. This he quickly unwrapped, tearing the
stuff away like a child playing pass the parcel. Underneath was
an elegant cherry-wood box. He pushed it slightly towards
Charlie. 'I'm only asking a thousand you understand. I'm barely
making a profit.' Charlie nodded. Mr Collins unwrapped a
mint and pushed it in his mouth. He took another gulp of tea.
'But I need the money, you see. An unexpectedly high tax bill.
Death and taxes Mr Thoroughgood.' Charlie's hand drifted
over the box's burnished brass catches.

'A thousand?'

'Yes, I really can't afford to go any lower.'

Charlie flicked the catch and raised the lid. Inside was a large glass bell jar, surrounded by black silk, nestling in a hollowed-out inversion of its own shape.

'Eight hundred then,' said Mr Collins. Charlie hadn't challenged his original price. The expanse of preserved skin visible through the glass was yellow in colour, buttery but dry like pastry. The thing's back. Charlie shut the lid. He looked at Mr Collins.

'Seven hundred and fifty. I will not go any lower.'

'The box is very beautiful.'

'Oh yes. Specially made. By its second owner. Shall we say seven fifty.' Collins breathing was shallow and excited.

'And where did you come by it?'

'An auction.'

'An auction!'

'Very recently. In Morocco. A private affair. For collectors.' Charlie touched the case. The wood was warm. Smooth as the silk lining inside.

'Seven fifty?'

'Cash,' said Collins, adding quickly 'if that's OK with you.' Charlie looked up at him, his grey-stubbled, flatiron-shaped face. The stained brim of his hat. No wife to care for him. Perhaps no friend in the world.

'I'm devoted to my collection. It pains me to part with anything. But items such as this can command too high a price.' Charlie nodded as he pulled open the drawer, withdrawing the cash box. 'A receipt. If you could make out a receipt. As proof of the sale.' Collins made a great fuss of the particulars. The spelling of his name and address, and the fullness of Charlie's own details. 'And if you could just sign there. Your signature at the bottom.' As Charlie handed him the paper, Collins seemed to lighten, his bones and muscles loosening, releasing knotted elements of himself. 'A fine transaction Mr Thoroughgood, a fine transaction. I'm sure it won't be long before you've sold the item on – at profit. Considerable profit.'

'I'm not selling it on,' said Charlie. Collins looked at him, surprised. 'This is for me.'

'What you got there?'

'Work,' said Charlie, clutching the bulky bag to his chest.

'Let's have a look.'

'Do you want a take-away?'

'Chuck. I'm trying to lose weight.' Charlie struggled up the stairs. The semi was small. Had become too small even for the two of them. Ten years of living there together and they had accumulated too much stuff. He made it on to the landing without her seeing what was in the large carrier bag. He'd wrapped the box inside a blanket. He couldn't have left it in the shop, the risk of a Trading Standards inspection discovering it amongst the stock. Besides it was his. He wanted it at home.

'I'll be down in a minute.' There was access to the loft in his room. A painted plywood panel that lifted up. He could keep it up there in its bag, wrapped in the blanket. She would never have to know. She was too fat to fit through the trapdoor. It was a risk bringing it home like this but he wanted to look at it, examine it properly. Something had kept him from doing so in the shop. He sat on the floor with his back against the door. If Janet tried to come in he would have enough time to push it under the blanket. He gathered some other, more innocuous items around himself. He unclipped the fastenings of the box. Who would have fashioned the item with such care? The bell-jar reflected the light fitting above it. Charlie shifted on his haunches. He reached into the box, feeling the smoothness of the silk against the back of his hands. Carefully, ensuring his grip was firm he extracted the glass case from its holding. There was a little rush of air as he did so, a crackle of static electricity. The thing's back was still facing him. He placed it down the on the carpet. Slowly, with two hands, he rotated the jar towards himself. The first thing he registered were its tiny hands, almost vestigial, like a dinosaur. He didn't want to look into its face. He'd expected the eyes to be closed, but they were open. Staring up at him. The sockets beneath were black. Impulsively he tapped on the glass. It sounded distinctively. Tink tink tink. The legs vibrated, curled into the dry, crispy belly. Each individual toe was discernible. The hair on its head was wispy and feathery, like a very old man's. He looked at it for a few moments longer then lifted the bell jar back into its box.

'Darling?'
　'Hmmm.'
　'Are you asleep.'
　'Hmmm.'
　'Chuck.' She knew he was cross about something. Knew he was sulking. He had waited downstairs, sat with his legs over the arm of the chair, flicking through the channels on the Freeview, listening to her preparations for bed. The clink of crockery going into the dishwasher, the boiling of the kettle, the water running into the bathroom sink. He'd let her climb the stairs, grunting that he'd be up in a minute. The Coué had already been placed in the loft, the beautiful cherry-wood box wrapped in a blanket. Eventually he ascended himself, sitting on the lavatory seat, running the electric toothbrush over his teeth. Now he lay in bed, pretending to have fallen immediately into a deep sleep. He thought about the night they first slept together. He hadn't wanted her then. She had chased him on to the bus, the number 21 via Killamarsh. He'd tried to tell her he didn't want to go out with her, didn't want to see her. But she'd chased him anyway and told him that she was going home

with him. And he'd assented. 'Let's have a look at you' she'd said as they lay naked, and he'd felt violated somehow, horribly exposed. He'd sworn to never let it happen again. But then it had. And one day he'd found himself feeling fonder about her. He'd veer between one and the other – the repulsion and the attraction. Part of him had craved it when she'd suggested moving in together. But somewhere, something inside him had vowed that he would not marry her. He didn't love her. He had to believe he could walk away. He wanted to know he could walk back to that past. Lying on the lawn. Just him. And dreams of his things. The things he loved. The life he loved.

'Darling?' She sounded sleepy now. This time he didn't even grunt. She desisted from questioning him. Outside, a lone car drove past, tyres rolling across the tarmac.

Later he woke. He couldn't see the time. The bulk of her body between him and the digital clock. It lit the room with a soft greenish tinge. The little house silent around him. And then somewhere above, a distant, percussive beat. It stopped. Was that what woke him? How could it? It seemed so quiet, so delicate. He lay, absolutely still, trying to hear the house around him, over Janet's heavy respiration. It came again. Precise and familiar. Tink, tink, tink. He stiffened, sat upright. Held his own breath, desperate to hear. The noise did not come again, unless that was it, starting up once more as sleep took him, like a beetle trapped in a cup. Tink. Tink. Tink.

Charlie was surprised when he arrived at the shop the next morning to find someone waiting for him once again. Except this time the figure wore uniform. A lone policeman. His first thought was that there'd been a break-in, or some trouble on the estate. His second, rather melodramatically was about the Coué, and he was grateful that he had taken it home, that it was safely hidden wrapped in the innocuous white blanket. But, it transpired, the visit was on account of another matter entirely.

'Do you recognise him?' The question repeated, a little too insistently, the policeman studying Charlie as he in turn studied the photo on the counter in front of him. It was Collins. Charlie thought about the Coué. Its tiny hands clasped to its desiccated chest.

'No,' he said, attempting to look the policeman straight in the eye. The man looked young to him. Bored. On a routine assignment.

'Are you sure sir?'

Charlie's Blackberry buzzed inside his jacket. He pulled it out but laid it on the counter without looking at it. 'Pretty sure. What's he done?'

'Died, sir.' This said dryly and without irony. Charlie peered at the photo again. He didn't want to speak but he tried to contort his face into an expression that said: 'maybe I did know him; let me have a better look.'

'He was found with your address in his wallet. There seemed no other reason for his presence in the area.'

'Ummm…'

'There is an independent witness who claims to have seen him hanging around the entrance to your shop, yesterday morning.'

'How did he die?'

'We found him at Victoria Quays.'

'Drowned?'

'No. He was at the water's edge but he hadn't jumped it. We don't know the cause of death.' The policeman studied Charlie. 'Yet.'

'It's him.' Charlie winced at the weakness of his own volte-face.

'So you do recognise him sir.'

'There was a man here yesterday. I thought he was mad. Or drunk. I sent him away.'

'What did he want?'

'He was selling. Or so he said. I wasn't interested.'

'So there was no transaction between you?'

'Oh no. It was all clearly dodgy. Furs. Ivory. Wouldn't touch it with a barge pole.' Charlie thought about the canal. Collins dropping dead.

'You bought nothing from him.'

'No. As I said. You're quite free to look around.'

'We found a large amount of cash on him.'

Charlie shrugged his shoulders. 'You're quite free to look around.' The policeman turned his head, looked around the shop at the hardwood display cases and pictures.

'I assume you have an alibi for your whereabouts last night.'

'What?'

The policeman turned back to look at Charlie. He couldn't have been more than thirty.

'Yes.' Charlie tried not to bristle too much. 'I was with my wife... my girlfriend. At home.' The policeman nodded.

'I just need to take some contact details then sir. If we need to speak to you again.'

Charlie left work early that day. He'd half-heartedly completed a number of orders, one of which needed parcel-posting to the US. He used the trip to the post office as an excuse to bunk off. Why was Collins dead? He had looked ill when Charlie had arrived. He wished he hadn't bought the thing off him now. Couldn't understand what pleasure he had thought owning it would bring. He sat in the car for a moment before starting it up. He noticed his heart was beating fast. There was a sense of being in trouble. As if he'd done something terribly wrong. But he hadn't. Collins was selling the thing. Charlie had bought it. He hadn't killed anyone. He would get rid of it. Throw it in the canal. And that would be the end of the matter. The garage beyond the windscreen suddenly seemed very dark. Something scratched in a corner. He turned on his headlamps, illuminating cobwebbed shelves.

Janet wasn't in when he got home. He took himself up to his room, suddenly not seeing the boxes with his exhibits in them, only the shadows between them. He turned on the two table-lamps and the angle-poise fastened to the bookshelf. Then he took a chair and stood on it, carefully lifting the square of painted plywood in the ceiling. Standing on his tip-toes he peered into the loft space. There was the box, still wrapped in its blanket, just where it had been the night before. He reached for it pulling it down into the room. He threw it onto the spare bed. It bounced for a moment before settling, making a slight depression in the centre of the duvet. Quickly, not wanting to, he uncoiled the blanket and lifted the catches on the box. The bell jar rested within, exactly as it had done when he had last looked at it. He turned it around, staring into the scrunched up face of the little thing inside. When he was a kid he had made himself shrunken heads for Halloween. Apples painted with clear nail-varnish with little faces carved in them. He had dried them in the airing cupboard. His simulations had been accurate. The face scowled. It looked furious. Or in pain. It had not moved since he had last looked at. Did he think that it would have done?

Janet had made dinner. Laid the table. He was thankful that she hadn't lit a candle.

'I'm sorry Chuck. I know you think I'm obsessed.'

'No.' It was a fish pie. She'd drawn lines in the mash potato with a fork before grilling it. He begun bisecting the lines across the grain with his own fork. Making little dashed slices. 'A man died today.'

'What? Who?'

'Last night. One of my suppliers.'

'Chuck. I'm sorry.'

'I didn't like him. Barely knew him.'

'Still. It throws you. How old was he?'

'He wasn't married.'

'Are you alright?' There was a pause. Charlie looked down at the tiny pieces of pie that he'd carved. He pushed a few of them across the plate, his fork scraping the china.

'I don't want to have a baby Janet,' he said, clearly, firmly. The central heating boiler clicked into life in the kitchen. He heard the roar of the gas. Imagined the flame burning blue. 'I don't love you,' he said, without looking at her.

He checked into the Pennine Way hotel. He'd stayed there before, when the water mains had burst. They both had. It would only be for a night or two. He lay back on the bed. The room smelt of air freshener and ancient cigars. He'd tried going to sleep with the television on, but sleep wouldn't come. Reluctantly, he turned the lights off. It wasn't dark. There was an illuminated strip beneath the doorway. Light came through the thin orange curtains. He must have dropped off for he awoke suddenly feeling panicky and disorientated. He didn't know where he was. He thought he saw something sitting on a chair in the corner of the room. Something little. Looking at him. He fumbled for the switch. Of course there was nothing apart from his balled up overcoat. The hotel seemed very quiet. A distant roar from the M1. Another noise started up, light and percussive. A repetitive tinkle. It seemed familiar, a beat he'd heard before. He closed his eyes and tried to ignore it. Except then it sounded as if it was outside his window. He was on the third floor. Nothing could get in. But then he remembered the front of the hotel. The extended block protruding into the car-park. He was reluctant to open the curtains. The rhythm became more insistent. Eventually he got out of the bed and threw the thin fabric aside. A heavy union flag shook in the wind, mounted on a portion of flat roof, just beyond the glass. Steel cable rattled against the metal eyelet sewn into its corner.

He'd put the Coué in the back of the car last night. He'd take it to the canal later in the morning. Maybe not the canal. Maybe the river. He'd take a canvas sack from the back of the shop, weigh the thing down with bricks. He looked over his shoulder as he slammed the car door shut. He was glad he could pull right into his garage. He hadn't felt safe when he'd walked out of the hotel this morning. Maybe the police had been watching him. It was ridiculous. How could he be a suspect in Collins' death.

A bottle toppled over somewhere in the darkness. He should clear the place out, now that the estate was emptying. He didn't want rats in the shop.

He found himself on the internet again all morning. There was an amount of work that he should be doing but he'd started a thread on one of the esoteria forums and wanted to watch its development.

Gothichost.net > Forum Index > General mythology

Chunnelgood
Member

Joined March 2001
Posts 271

Posted Fri Feb 11, 2006, 9:08 am Post subject Coué facts

Wondered if anyone had any experience or any knowledge about the Coué or any related stories? Anyone know of anybody who owns or has owned a Coué?

– – –

Turglover
Member

Joined Feb 2003
Posts 64

Posted Fri Feb 11, 2006, 10:11 am Post subject Coué facts

You joke with me Chunnelgood man right. There ain't no such thing as a Coué

Life is a waste of time, time is a waste of time. Get wasted all of the time and you"ll have the time of your life!

Chunnelgood
Member

Joined March 2001
Posts 271

Posted Fri Feb 11, 2006, 10:15 am Post subject Coué facts

Coué does exist. Have seen photographs. That aside wondered if anyone had any stories or knew any mythology.

– – –

Eldritch Nut-cache
Member

Joined August 2002
Posts 98

Posted Fri Feb 11, 2006, 9:08 am Post subject Coué facts

The Coué destroys. Takes from you. He who owns the Coué carries the weight.

'Ten million ships on fire. The entire Dalek race wiped out in one second... I watched it happen. I MADE it happen!'

Turglover
Member

Joined Feb 2003
Posts 64

Posted Fri Feb 11, 2006, 10:33 am Post subject Coué facts

You ain't seen no photographs man. F**k that s**t!!!

Life is a waste of time, time is a waste of time. Get wasted all of the time and you''ll have the time of your life!

Chunnelgood
Member

Joined March 2001
Posts 271

Posted Fri Feb 11, 2006, 10:37 am Post subject Coué facts

Eldritch. What is the weight you carry if you own the Coué?

– – –

Eldritch Nut-cache
Member

Joined August 2002
Posts 98

Posted Fri Feb 11, 2006, 9:08 am Post subject Coué facts

The Coué was made to take. It draws it out of you like salt draws water. It feeds on that which you love the most.

_____

'Ten million ships on fire. The entire Dalek race wiped out in one second... I watched it happen. I MADE it happen!'

_____

Turglover
Member

Joined Feb 2003
Posts 64

Posted Fri Feb 11, 2006, 10:58 am Post subject Coué facts

You guys crack me up.

_____

Life is a waste of time, time is a waste of time. Get wasted all of the time and you"ll have the time of your life!

_____

Charlie wondered how quickly he could find a buyer. It wasn't something that he could go on the open market with.

Anyway he would pay to get rid of the thing. He remembered how carefully Collins had made him fill out the receipt. The patient requests for exact details. It couldn't be a simple matter of just dumping it. If that had been the case Collins would have dropped it in the canal himself. He wondered how carefully Collins had selected him – how much research he'd done. Had Charlie been the perfect candidate? He felt as if he didn't have that luxury himself. He needed to be rid of the Coué and now. Every second between him and being free of it felt as if it multiplied the danger. Danger? Danger of what? He looked around the shop – the neatly arranged cases, the patchwork colours of the exhibits within. The plethora of items carefully ordered on shelves and bookcases. The room felt very dark. Charlie switched on an extra light.

You would think it would be easy to divest yourself of something. Anything. Smash it up. Burn it. Bury it. But to transfer ownership. That was another matter. He decided to go for a walk around the estate.

To the left of the concourse two shaven-headed boys kicked a tennis ball back and forth between them. Not yet teenagers they had an air of brutality about them. They didn't look up as he passed. Their ball thumped repeatedly against the brickwork. A glacial February wind blew. Charlie pulled himself into the wall. Another sound came towards him, echoing off the high concrete. A distant percussive tapping. Something hard against glass. It shared the rhythm of the boys' ball. There was the charity shop on the far side of the estate, where it met the main road. If he went to them with a pre-printed form – he could knock it up on the computer – they would only have to sign. A record of ownership having passed. He was sure he could convince them. He turned a corner into one of the walkways – a narrow flyover that ran above the service road beneath. It was long and narrow, fashioned from dirty concrete and breezeblocks. He tried to walk as fast as he could. The wind caught some litter behind him. A glass bottle rolled across the pathway, or so it sounded. It must have had a lump on it, some irregularity. It sounded each time it struck the ground. Tink, tink, tink. Something struck Charlie in the chest. Something come to life, caught in his clothes. His Blackberry. He'd set it to email him if the message board was updated. He carried on walking as he pulled it out, running the thumbwheel down.

S
Guest

Joined Feb 2006
Posts 1

Posted Fri Feb 11, 2006, 11:57 am Post subject Coué facts
The Coué is not the thing. The Coué was made to make something else. The Coué merely calls for it.

Charlie had had enough of this now. He put the Blackberry back in his pocket. He was taking the necessary action. And then he'd be done with it.

It was all superstitious nonsense. Ridiculous, superstitious nonsense. The appeal of his collection was in its irony, not its mythic heritage. He had no interest in magical thinking. He pushed open the door to the charity shop. He had been in a number of times before, just in case he might uncover an item of real value. Such accidental finds were rare, but did happen. He spent a moment at a rail of peppery-smelling clothes, flicking across the brown faded jackets and wrinkled, off-white shirts. Then he approached the old woman behind the cash-register, who was occupied flattening out some metallic wrapping paper.

'Is there an Esme works here?' said Charlie, as convincingly as he could manage.

'Sorry love?'

'Does Esme work here? I had something for her.'

'I only come in of a Monday.' The woman wasn't interested in Charlie. The paper was far more interesting to her.

'I had an item for her. A box I'd promised she could sell on. Could I bring it round for her later?'

'Do what you like love.'

'That's very kind of you. What's your name?'

The woman looked up at him again. Her skin looked as grey as her hair. She might have been fifty or seventy. It depended on her diet, how much she drank.

'Juliet,' she said. She eyed him suspiciously.

'Not Juliet Gardener.' For a minute Charlie thought she wouldn't take the bait.

'Forester.'

'Forester.'

'I don't know you,' said the old woman indignantly.

'Christopher. Christopher Trace. I'll be back with it shortly.' He smiled, in as friendly manner as he could.

It felt like it was getting dark when he got back to the shop. He didn't want to go into the garage to get the thing. He left the door open when normally he might shut it, allowing what pale daylight there was to disperse the shadows. He hurriedly retrieved the paper bag from the boot.

He didn't want to look at it again. He didn't even want to take off the blanket. He went about creating the document first. There was no need for it to be complicated.

'I Charles Louis Thoroughgood transfer all rights of ownership of this

item to Juliet Forester this 11th day of February 2006.'

He printed the paper out. The thought occurred to him, what if Juliet opened – or one of the other women and on finding the document were so horrified at the dreadful thing that they called the police. He went and retrieved his toolbox from the back office.

He removed the bell jar, keeping the Coué turned away from him. With a scalpel he carefully worked a piece of the black silk away from the wood. Then using a small bit on the power drill he hollowed-out a shallow well in the exposed mahogany. He cut the printed document into a small strip, containing the text, rolling it into a pellet. Delicately he inserted the pellet into the well and filled it with epoxy resin. Then he reattached the silk, using a small dab of Magna-tac. He left it to dry. Of course this was all ridiculous. He was merely doing it for his peace of mind.

He found another box, a cardboard box. He placed the blanket wrapped bundle inside and taped the whole package up tightly. In block-capitals, on the side, he wrote 'Esme'.

He drove round to the main road. He was worried the woman would be gone and he would find the charity shop all locked up. But it was still open, fluorescent-lights flickering painfully. He insisted on carrying the box through into the back. Wouldn't hear of Juliet carrying it. He was relying on her fecklessness. As he had hoped she stayed at her till, reading her *Sheffield Star* and eating Maltesers. The chaotic nature of the stock room was a gift. There was an old wardrobe in the corner. Checking the door as he went, Charlie hurriedly pushed a table across the room and stood on it, chucking the box on top of the wardrobe and pushing it back as far as he could against the wall. He leapt down, pulled the table back to its original position and satisfied himself that the box could not be seen from the floor. It was perfectly possible that it might stay there unnoticed for several years.

There was nothing immoral about his actions because it was all just nonsense. He had achieved peace of mind. He had divested himself of the vile item. He had spoken the truth to Janet. Everything was clean.

He thought he would stay in the shop for a while. He might search online for some temporary accommodation, somewhere to rent until he and Janet had resolved what to do with the house. He clicked on Firefox and began to type in Google. As he did the address bar brought up a list of other sites, Gothichost being the uppermost. Idly he scrolled down and clicked. Feeling freer now he was curious to see how the chat might have progressed.

Eldritch Nut-cache
Member

Joined August 2002
Posts 98

Posted Fri Feb 11, 2006, 9:08 am Post subject Coué facts

The Coué was made to take. It draws it out of you like salt draws water. It feeds on that which you love the most.

'Ten million ships on fire. The entire Dalek race wiped out in one second... I watched it happen. I MADE it happen!'

Turglover
Member

Joined Feb 2003
Posts 64

THE COUÉ

Posted Fri Feb 11, 2006, 10:58 am Post subject Coué facts

You guys crack me up.

Life is a waste of time, time is a waste of time. Get wasted all of the time and you"ll have the time of your life!

S
Guest

Joined Feb 2006
Posts 1

Posted Fri Feb 11, 2006, 11:57 am Post subject Coué facts
The Coué is not the thing. The Coué was made to make something else. The Coué merely calls for it.

– – –

Finton3000
Member

Joined Feb 2002
Posts 112

Posted Fri Feb 11, 2006, 12:17 am Post subject Coué facts

Correct. The Mother that bred it. It's black with hate.

'Oh no tears please, it's a waste of good suffering'

His phone went. It was Janet. He switched it off. For the first time in the day he thought about her. Felt the tension in his stomach. But he was relieved. Relieved to be alone. He would go out in a minute. The off-licence would be open. He might buy himself a bottle of wine. There was only one thing left that irritated him. Why had Collins died? He stopped the thoughts, ceasing them with his will. The curse was nonsensical. Besides, Collins had already sold the thing. Surely he should have been free. Of course he was free. He had always been free. The man just died. That was all.

Janet put down the phone. He wasn't going to answer was he? Let that be it then. She didn't believe him though. She knew Charlie. Knew that he didn't know his own mind. His own heart. She went down to the kitchen and turned on the light. What she saw was black, like a bat and taller than her. It shouldn't have been able to move the way it did. She screamed so hard it hurt her throat. And then it was on her, so no one would have heard a thing.

Saturday Mary

EMMA UNSWORTH

The first time she saw Gabriel he was on his hands and knees, picking up pieces of broken brown glass from under the benches. *Thanks*, she said. He smiled and showed the gap from a tooth he'd lost in a fall.

At 3am the club was almost tidy. She was one of twelve working there, wasting away the long, black hours beneath a glitter ball sun that spun slowly to tick flecks of light around the cavernous rooms. Her skin was pale, almost translucent, like that of the blind cave fish in the city's museum. Her hair hung in bluish strips around her face, although it might have been the light. In an opal vest top and faded out jeans she glowed in the dark. Not that anyone noticed. It wasn't that kind of place.

She was surprised by his smile. Its *simplicity*. The crowd tonight had been angry about the prices, the plastic tumblers, the wait. Anything and everything.

'What time do you get off?' one man had yelled and she'd rolled her eyes. 'Don't worry, I'm not chatting you up,' he'd said. 'I'm going to wait outside and fuck you up.'

Those that hadn't shouted had tried to slip their hot sweaty hands down the back of her jeans as she collected empties and wiped out the ashtrays. In the toilet, alone, she had banged her head hard against the wall and felt better.

Gabriel stood up and put the shards of dirty glass into the bin bag she was holding. She noticed that his hands were perfect and he wore a single gemstone ring.

'Thanks,' she said again. He turned and went, his long coat sweeping after him, in between various teenagers intently mopping and brushing the vast floor.

The next day she dreamt that the floor of the club fell through to the foundations, its rotten edges finally giving way, punters screaming and twisting amongst bottle tops and cigarette ends.

She was disappointed when he didn't appear for a week. She didn't tell a soul. She sketched his face over and over onto beer mats and bought a long coat, which she wore with the collar up and badges on her shoulder. She thought about him as she walked around the club, dodging the arguments and fights, squinting when the spotlights flashed her way.

The club was underground. It made it difficult to get people out, when they'd had too much. The bouncers didn't really care, and she had to admit she didn't either, as they dragged each deadbeat up the stairs and dumped them onto the street. She'd skip back down the stairway skidding her shoes in the piss, shit and sick that lay in a thick line, like the trail of some monstrous slug.

The night Gabriel reappeared, she'd pretty much given up on ever seeing him again. She felt so despondent arriving in work that she secretly dropped a shot of brandy into a coffee mug and drank it straight down. Stealing wasn't something she usually did, and she was ashamed that she'd allowed herself to be pushed into it. Another shot and she could almost laugh. Three shots later she was able to maintain a heady dignity whilst serving the most aggressive of men.

'Hey, I gave you a twenty, you fucking bitch.'

There were no twenties in the till.

'Don't look at me like that. You fucking bitch. I gave you a twenty.'

All in all she stole so much brandy that on her break she could barely walk to the dance floor. She staggered there gradually, clinging to the slimy pillars for support. Someone spilled their drink down her skirt.

On the dance floor, she danced until she felt the buzzing move through her ears and into her whole head. Her limbs rotated without much rhythm and there was a certain paralysis to her face. She looked up to the ceiling and saw red neon devils stretching away into darkness. She reached her fingers up to touch them and someone grabbed her hand.

'Mind if I cut in?'

She lowered her head and saw Gabriel.

'I dance as I dream,' she said.

He turned in his coat. The lights moved away from her and she felt suddenly lost.

'No! Don't leave me.'

He took her hand again. She gripped his tight and could feel the coolness of the metal ring between her fingers.

'Where are we going?'

'Away.'

'From what?''

'These *people*.'

He put his arm around her and guided her through the packed club. When they got to the stairs she put her head under his coat. It smelled of fresh bedding, chlorine, leafmulch. She watched his boots to know when to step.

Round the corner, she thought he might kiss her, but he put his hands in his pockets and brought his coat out wide on either side. She smiled and swayed, coming to rest against a wall. His eyes on her were bright and constant. He took her hand again and led her to the other side of town, along roads strewn with kebab shops and empty taxis, until the streets got narrower, older, and she didn't recognise the names.

They stopped outside an unmarked door. It was a bar she'd never heard of, a tiny place tucked away under railway arches. The bricks around the door were crumbly, separated above the door by a pockmarked wooden beam.

There was nobody in except the barman.

'Evening, Gabriel,' he said.

She sat down at a table near the back and checked the shape of her hair in the shiny tiles that were level with her head. This was a nice place. There were pictures of ships hung on the wall, brass lamps, velvet curtains. Different types of glasses. A real fire.

Gabriel bought all the drinks, although she didn't once see him pay. They drank shots and slammers, sweet and sour little mouthfuls that burned down her throat and made her want to sing.

'One condition,' Gabriel said, after their seventh tequila. 'You have to stay and talk to me until morning.'

'I have a condition, too,' she said. 'I was born with a broken heart.'

'Yes,' he replied slowly, getting up to go to the bar. 'That sort of thing.'

An hour later they were running along the street, taking play punches at each other. She hit his arm and he grinned wildly. He was running in a straight line but missed her every time. Any minute now, he'll take me home, she thought. He'll take me home and there'll be holding and staring and I'll be in love again for a while. So when he hailed a cab all that really surprised her was the time on the dashboard. It was suddenly morning. She looked at Gabriel's face and saw wrinkles where he smiled, spokes around his eyes. He had a look of great age about him. And then she felt sick and had to slide down the window to let in some air.

His flat was north of the city and the cab stopped opposite a boarded up building that had a ramshackle sign saying *Trust Centre*. Mary felt hollow inside, more hollow than ever before.

It was a dead zone, his street – littered with waste paper and plastic, and lined with leafless trees. Things were moved around by the elements here; nothing moved itself.

Gabriel got the cab. The steering wheel slid through the driver's hands. Mary turned around and stared and stared at the tall grey Y-shaped streetlights, splitting into two against the sky, like birds drawn by a child.

The cab chugged away. The block of flats was before them. They picked their way down the muddy path. It was scrubby and uneven and tangled with brambles that reached to scratch her tights. He pushed open the door. They climbed nine flights, up and up until she almost felt sober.

His flat had no door at all. A single window channeled the sky's pale light onto the floorboards. The walls were patterned with patches of damp. She heard a shuffle somewhere.

Gabriel sat down on a ripped leather armchair. She immediately got on her knees before him. She unbuttoned his coat and searched for the fastening on his trousers. He cupped her chin in his hand and brought his head down level with hers. His face was smooth against her cheek.

'What do you want?' he whispered in her ear.

She closed her eyes and sighed. Before she knew it, she was crying. He moved back to look at her and smudged her tears away with his thumbs.

'Life or death?' he asked.

'What?'

His eyes were black now and she understood.

'Death,' she said quickly.

The window looked out towards the city. She could see the quiet dawn road stretching back there, its railings strapped with soaked carnations, cellophane glinting. The ledge was hard under her feet, so much harder than his hands. And then she felt the night air catch in her throat, the cold thrill of falling, the death kicking away inside of her.

When the sirens shortly cut through the hush, it was as though Gabriel had never been there. There were just police officers, who wouldn't believe that she didn't do it. And her boyfriend, Joe, who wished that he'd done it to her instead.

Lancashire

NICHOLAS ROYLE

'Nelson, Colne, Darwen,' said Cassie, reading the names off the roadsigns. 'I remember all these Lancashire towns from Bournemouth,' she said.

'Your mam's talking nonsense again,' said her husband Paul into the rear-view mirror.

'What are you talking about, Mummy?' asked James, who at ten was the elder of the two. His two front teeth still hadn't closed the gap, freckles scattered across his nose.

'From when I worked in the sorting office in Bournemouth one Christmas,' Cassie explained.

'For Christmas... yeah...' began Ellie, James's younger sister, 'I want an iPod Nano. A black one.'

Ellie, her naturally streaked hair looking like it needed a good brush, enunciated slowly, as if she still couldn't quite believe she could speak. Or was Paul projecting his own wonder at his daughter's power of speech? She had been able to speak for years, of course, but had indeed been a slow starter.

'You can't have one,' said her brother.

'Why not?'

'Because I haven't got one.'

'You've got one on your Christmas list. I saw it.'

'But I haven't got one *yet* and you can't get one at the same time as I get one. You have to wait till I've had one for six weeks. Or a year.'

'No, I don't. Mummy, do I?'

'That's enough,' said Cassie, smiling at Paul. 'Look at the wonderful scenery. Isn't this lovely? Just imagine. If we'd been driving for half an hour from our old house, we wouldn't even have got beyond the North Circular.'

James and Ellie ignored this, bent over PSP and Gameboy respectively, articulating their thumbs in ways their parents had never learned to do. Paul wondered how long it would be before Ellie decided she also had to graduate from a Gameboy to a PSP.

Sunlight flashed across the windscreen, sparkling in a scattering of raindrops and temporarily blinding him.

'Are you keeping your eye on the map?' he asked Cassie.

'Just keep going on the A666,' said Cassie. 'All the way.'

'Right through Blackburn?' he asked, blinking.

'Right on past these dark Satanic mills,' she said as they passed another refurbished chimney.

'Mummy?'

'Do you know what I read the other day?' said Paul. 'I read that "dark Satanic mills" was never meant to imply this sort of thing –' he waved his hand at yet another converted mill – 'the industrial revolution and all that. What Blake was really talking about, apparently, were Oxford and Cambridge universities.'

'Mummy?'

'What, darling?'

'What does Satanic mean?'

'Oh, really, Paul?' said Paul, mimicking Cassie. 'That's fascinating, Paul. Thank you for sharing that, Paul.'

'Ask your dad, Ellie. He seems to know all about it.' Cassie placed her hand on Paul's leg and smiled at him. 'It was fascinating, darling. I didn't know that, actually.'

'It's only conjecture, of course.'

'Are we nearly there?' asked James.

'That's a good question,' said Cassie, looking at Paul. '*Are* we nearly there?'

'You tell me. You've got the map.' Paul's lips straightened into a suppressed smile.

Conversation was soon restricted to the essentials of navigation while they negotiated Blackburn.

'Who are we going to see again?' James asked as they found their way back on to the main road.

'Penny and Howard. Friends of your mam's.'

'Howard and Penny, friends of your dad's more like,' said Cassie.

'I thought we were going to see Connor,' said James.

'We are,' said Paul. 'Connor is Penny and Howard's son.'

'Are those the people we met in the park?' James asked.

'You know they are. Now, shush, matey. I've got to read the signs.'

'Your dad needs all his concentration to read the signs. A lot of men find it very, very hard reading signs.'

Paul smiled, then frowned at a hidden sign.

'What did that say? Did that say Wilpshire?'

They turned off the A666 and within a couple of minutes pulled up outside a well-kept Victorian semi. Pampas grasses grew in the lawned garden, steps led up to the front door. Paul pulled on the handbrake.

'Paul, I hope this is going to be all right,' Cassie said quietly. 'I mean, we barely know these people.'

'It's a little late for that,' Paul answered.

'We've been out with them, what, twice for drinks?'

'You know what they say about pampas grasses, don't you?' Paul muttered.

'What?' came James's voice from the back.

'Never you mind,' said Paul. 'It'll be fine. Penny's into stained glass, remember. If you run out of things to talk about, just talk about stained glass. Did you know, kids, that your mam's in the *Guinness Book of Records* for length of time talking about stained glass.'

'What about you and Howard?' asked Cassie with an indulgent smile.

'We'll have something in common. Didn't he say he liked punk and new wave? Late 70s, 80s music? Anyway, no one expects blokes to talk. We just have to sit there looking like we're not having a shit time. Anyway,' he added, 'it's more for the children, isn't it? They liked Connor when they met him. And it's kind of them to invite us. Perhaps they know what it's like to be new to an area.'

At that point, Cassie became aware of the front door opening and Penny and Howard appearing, all smiles. The child, Connor, squeezed between their legs and ran down the path towards them.

'Here goes,' she said as she opened the car door.

They got the standard tour.

Downstairs rooms tastefully restored, with an attractive archway ('Looks original. I don't know, maybe 1920s') connecting them. Kitchen long and narrow – 'We're going to open it up at the back – here and here – and have lovely big French windows where that corner is,' said Penny. 'It's lovely how it is,' flattered Cassie. 'What, all this clinker? Tongue and groove? Ugh.' And so it went on. Upstairs, Connor's bedroom ('Is this really my room?' Strange child. Though weren't all children strange, apart from your own, Cassie thought), amazingly tidy for a ten-year-old's; Penny and Howard's room, drawers and wardrobes neatly closed; and a tiny office for Penny ('Oh, you know, PR,' she said with a modest, almost dismissive wave of the hand, when asked to remind them what she did) – a filing cabinet, a laptop closed on a little table, a suspiciously tidy desk-tidy, a pile of magazines (*Lancashire Life*, *Closer*, *OK*). And finally the converted attic, double bed, fresh towels. Velux windows – 'You can see Blackpool Tower on a good day.'

It wasn't a good day.

Back downstairs a bottle of Pinot Grigio was opened for Cassie and Penny, and local beers broken out for the boys.

'Boys,' said Penny with a little laugh.

The children had stayed upstairs with Connor.

'Is this Wire?' Paul asked, glancing at the stereo. 'Early Wire, by the sound of it.'

'Yeah, it's *Pink Flag*,' said Howard.

'Oh, they're off,' said Penny, leaning towards Cassie on the leather sofa and dropping her hand briefly on her knee.

Flashes of red and green lit up the sky outside the window, followed by a bang.

'It's not bonfire night yet, is it?' asked Paul.

'We've not had Halloween yet,' Cassie said.

'I remember when fireworks were saved until Guy Fawkes' Night and Halloween was neither here nor there,' said Howard.

'Mmm,' agreed Paul. 'Nice beer,' he added, holding his glass up to the halogen lighting to admire its golden-brown colour.

Howard passed him the bottle.

'Pendle Witches' Brew,' Paul read from the label.

'Pendle Hill's just up the road,' Howard offered.

'It's very good of you to invite us over,' Paul heard Cassie saying to Penny.

'We know what it's like when you've just moved somewhere new,' Penny said in response.

'It was weird that day in the park,' Cassie remembered. 'The way you and I met at exactly the same time as Howard and Paul bumped into each other right over the other side of the park.'

'I remember you had Ellie with you in the playground,' said Penny, 'and I assumed it was just the two of you. Then you told me your husband and son were somewhere kicking a football. And a minute later they turned up – with Howard and Connor.'

'What were you doing there anyway,' Cassie asked, 'so far from home?'

There was a moment's silence. Paul looked up and saw Penny staring into her wine glass.

'We'd just been for a walk, hadn't we, darling? In Fletcher Moss Gardens,' said Howard.

'Mmm, of course,' said Penny, getting to her feet. 'I'm just going to check on the hotpot.'

'Lancashire hotpot!' exclaimed Paul in delight.

'Is there any other kind?'

'So, have you not been here long?' Cassie asked Howard.

'Oh dear, is it that obvious?' Howard said, and Paul saw Cassie colour up. 'No, we haven't been here that long, hence the drive down to south Manchester to investigate Fletcher Moss. We're still seeing the sights.'

'I think I'll go and see if Penny wants a hand,' said Cassie, and Paul raised his glass to his lips to hide his look of dismay.

'Lovely house,' he said, his eyes scanning the walls. There were a handful of pictures, but they were beyond bland, the sort of thing you might buy for a fiver in IKEA. 'Do you mind?' he asked as he got up and walked over to check out the CD collection.

'Go ahead. A lot of stuff's still in storage. That's just what I couldn't bear to be parted from.'

Joy Division, The Cure, Buzzcocks, UK Subs.

'What's your favourite Cure album?' he asked Howard.

'Oh, I don't know. Remind me which ones are up there.'

'*Seventeen Seconds, Pornography, Faith, Disintegration...*'

'Er, I really don't know. *Disintegration*, perhaps.'

'Mm-hmm. "The Hanging Garden" is an amazing track, isn't it?'

'Fantastic.'

Paul moved away from the CD collection and noticed

an Ordnance Survey map folded up on the mantelpiece.

'I love OS maps,' he said. 'Can I have a look?'

'Of course.'

Paul spread the map out on the coffee table. The conurbations of Blackburn, Accrington and Burnley looked like clots in the green lungs of Lancashire.

'Can you see Barnoldswick?' Howard asked, kneeling down next to Paul. 'See how big it is considering it's not even on an A-road? That's because of the Rolls-Royce factory.'

'Oh, right.'

'All these little villages here –' Howard pointed to the section of the map between Burnley and the moors above Hebden Bridge – 'the roads just run into the hills and stop. Interesting places. Lots of unusual traditions and rituals…'

'Really?' Paul was interested, but they heard Penny calling everyone from the kitchen.

The children came running downstairs. Paul caught James and gave him a bear hug. As the boy struggled to get free, Paul ruffled his hair.

'Good kids,' Howard said.

'Yeah, we're lucky. They leapt at the chance to come here so they could see Connor again.'

Howard's lips stretched over his teeth in an approximation of a smile.

In the converted attic, Paul and Cassie lay side by side. Cassie was reading a Jackie Kay collection; in an effort to meet some new people, she had joined a book club. Paul was making inroads into a thriller by Stephen Gallagher but was finding it hard to concentrate.

'Cassie?'

'Hmm?' Not looking up.

'Don't you think they're a bit odd? Howard and Penny. Don't you think there's something about them that's not quite right?'

'Hmm?'

'I'm serious.'

Finally, Cassie looked up. She closed her book but kept her place with a thumb.

'You've had too much to drink.'

'I only had two beers.'

'That second one was quite strong.'

'Do you know what it was called? It was called Nightmare. Can you believe it?'

'Another local brew?' There was a faintly patronising tone in Cassie's voice, as if she regarded the interest in local beers as endearing, a 'boy' thing.

'It's actually from Yorkshire, but Yorkshire's just up the road. Something to do with the Legend of the White Horse.'

'I hope it doesn't *give* you nightmares.'

'I felt at times tonight as if I might be having one, actually.'

'Was the hotpot a bit too fatty for you?'

'That was all right. It was the warm salad with black pudding I wasn't sure about.'

'Faddy. I think Penny and Howard are very nice and they've been very kind.'

'There's just something about them. It's hard to put my finger on. Howard thought "The Hanging Garden" by the Cure was on *Disintegration*, but it's not. It's on *Pornography*.'

'Big deal.' A little impatience was starting to creep into Cassie's voice.

'But these were CDs he said he couldn't bear to be parted from. I just got the impression they were trying a bit too hard to get us to like them. Or trust them.'

'Don't be silly. We just have some shared interests. Like stained glass.'

Paul laughed. 'I thought you and Penny were never going to shut up about stained glass at the dinner table.'

'Common interests, that's all it is. Now do you think we

could get some sleep? They said they'd show us a bit of the countryside in the morning.'

But sleep was a long time coming, for Paul at least.

Paul wanted his dream to continue. In fact, he was convinced it would continue with or without him. The question was whether he could remain part of it. His journey towards full consciousness became a struggle between his strong attachment to the dream – the grammar and meaning of which were losing coherence by the second – and his acknowledgement of responsibility. The day, he sensed, was bringing anxiety, though from what quarter he did not know. Within a few more seconds the warp of reality had completely overpowered the weft of the dream and Paul felt a sudden, inexplicable panic. He sat up and hurriedly pulled on his clothes. Cassie woke and asked him what the matter was, but he couldn't bring himself to answer.

Seconds later he was taking the stairs two at a time down to the next floor, where the children had slept in Connor's bedroom. He opened the door. The room was as quiet as the rest of the house. The curtains were still drawn and the room was dark, but he saw instantly that not only was the bed empty, but the two sleeping bags were as well, left untidily where they lay like the discarded casings of chrysalises.

Paul backed out on to the landing and descended swiftly to the ground floor. Marching down the hall as if wading through treacle, he glanced into the living room, which looked no livelier than the bedroom, and approached the closed door that led to the kitchen. He watched as his hand reached out to open it and the next thing he saw was Penny standing at the sink and beyond her were James and Ellie sat at the table eating croissants and *pains au chocolat* with Connor. All three had chocolate rings around their mouths.

Paul felt confused and relieved at the same time. He said hello and accepted Penny's offer of a pot of tea and retreated, saying he would be back down in a minute. As he passed the living room he saw Howard bent over the coffee table studying the map.

'Morning,' said Howard.

'Hi.'

As Paul climbed the stairs, he tried to calm himself down, as there was clearly no sense in sharing any of this with Cassie. She met him on the first-floor landing and they went back down to the kitchen together.

Once breakfast was over and the children were dressed, everyone moved towards the front door. Paul and Cassie stepped onto the garden path. Paul took the bags to the car, while Cassie waited for the children. He packed the boot and leaned against the car, enjoying the view over the fields and feeling sheepish for his strange behaviour and yet pretty good about everything, considering. He took in a deep breath and let it out slowly, enjoying the purely physical sensation of filling and emptying his lungs. Over there were Blackburn, Accrington and Burnley, yet he could see nothing but green.

Cassie joined him and told him that the children wanted to go in Connor's car.

'Fine,' he said and opened the driver's door to get in.

'Their car's around the back,' Cassie said.

'No problem. We wait here, yeah?'

Cassie nodded and Paul looked in the rear-view mirror. It didn't matter how much the children might occasionally bicker in the back of the car, when they weren't there he missed them.

Two or three minutes went by and Howard and Penny still hadn't shown up. Paul kept checking the rear-view mirror.

'How long does it take to strap three kids into a car?' he asked.

Cassie shook her head.

'They're probably arguing over who sits where,' she said. 'You know what they're like.'

'Not usually when it's someone else's car,' said Paul. 'I daresay Howard's a safe driver,' he added after a moment.

Cassie, who knew what was going through Paul's mind, said, 'How do *you* drive when you have someone else's child in the back? Recklessly or even more safely than usual?'

'Yeah, you're right. As usual,' he said, with a little smile. 'But what's taking them so long?'

They waited a further minute then Paul got out of the car and wandered down to the lane that led to the back of the house. There was no sign of a vehicle making its way down towards him, so he had a quick look back at Cassie sitting in their car and started walking up the lane. He reached a track on the left, which could only be the access to the rear of Howard and Penny's house. Still no sign of their car. He ran down the little track towards the back of their house, which he isolated from its neighbours. There was no car. He looked around wildly, suddenly feeling exactly as he had done upon waking when he had been convinced, for whatever reason, that the children were no longer in the house.

At his feet in the mud was a set of tyre tracks. They led towards the lane and then turned left rather than right.

There had to be another way around to the front of the house. He turned right and ran back to the road, where Cassie was still sitting waiting in the car.

'Have you seen them?' he asked breathlessly as he reached the car.

'What do you mean?'

'The car's gone. They've gone. They've all gone. They've got the children!'

'Maybe they're coming another way round?'

'They're not. They'd have been here by now. They've gone and they've taken the children. I don't know why, but they've taken the children. Oh Jesus Christ!'

They looked at each other and for a moment said nothing. Paul's breath froze in the air in little clouds.

'Call the police,' said Cassie. 'No, wait. Maybe they're still in the house? They got delayed or they're playing a joke.'

'There's no car at the back.'

'Let's check the house.'

Together they ran up the front path. The door was locked so Paul knocked hard. When no one came he put his elbow through the stained glass and reached inside to open the door. They entered the house. Paul ran upstairs. Cassie checked the living room and the kitchen. Something made her open cupboard doors in the kitchen. The cupboards were empty. There was no food, nor were there any pots and pans other than the ones they had used the night before. She ran into the living room, where she remembered seeing an oak cabinet with closed doors. It too was empty.

'Paul!' she shouted upstairs.

'Cassie!' he shouted from above. 'Come up here!'

She ran upstairs.

'Look!' he said.

The filing cabinet in Penny's office was empty. The laptop had disappeared from the table. The desk tidy was as suspiciously tidy as before. In the bedroom that they had said was theirs, the wardrobes contained nothing but a few rattling wire hangers. In Connor's room it was the same story. Drawers filled with stale air. Empty cupboards that they had presumed were stuffed with toys.

No one lived in this house. No one at all.

The Foster Parents

PAUL MAGRS

He was a twitchy man who lived next door. He was all white. He'd glare at you from under these bushy eyebrows. His wife was plump and friendly-looking, but she seemed scared of everything and you'd get no more than a squeak out of her.

'Hello, Mrs Foster,' I'd say, if we passed on the street or if I saw her over the garden fence.

'Squeak,' she'd say, and hurry on by.

It was that man. It was as if he'd beaten her and made her like this. She was all quivering flesh and he was hard, hard bone.

Robert and I like to be neighbourly. Not too much so. But just so's you know people are there, in case of emergencies, or for a little drink at Christmas. The Fosters from next door had been round for precisely one sweet sherry one Boxing Day and their company hadn't been exactly scintillating. 'You've put an old-fashioned fireplace back,' Mr Foster scowled. 'We have a new gas fire. Wood-effect surround.'

'Squeak,' added Mrs Foster, and finished off her sherry in one go.

They never came round again. Not the Christmas following, nor ever since. And, of course, we never received any such invite from them.

We'd hear raised voices sometimes, through the walls. Not that we made a habit of listening. Oddly, we would hear her voice raised above the level of her husband's. She would scream and squeak extremely loudly sometimes. Something about that noise made me shudder. But what can you do? You can't interfere in other people's lives.

Nobody else ever went into or came out of their house. At least, not until about a year ago. When all that business started, it came as a shock. Comings and goings at all hours. The front door banging. Children running down the front path. I don't suppose anyone else noticed the changes. The Fosters live in the end-terrace house and we are their closest neighbours. Our little street and the surrounding streets are full of busy comings-and-goings. These new children and teenagers wouldn't have stood out as very conspicuous.

But they did to us.

We had assumed the Fosters were as childless as we were. I think one of us had even asked them, on that uncomfortable Boxing Day occasion. I swear I can remember Mr Foster twisting up his face at the very idea of having children. And I think she, in turn, looked sad.

So that was why it struck me as extremely odd, that day last August, when I saw the twins step out of the Fosters' front door.

We were setting off in the car for a few days in the Lake District. We find it very peaceful up there. Robert enjoys driving around those very steep and bendy roads in the mountains. We often go for a weekend and it can be quite reasonably priced. So we had loaded up the car and we had locked up the house and we were at the point where we were about to drive off. 'Did you check the bathroom window locks?' Robert asks. 'Did you switch off the toaster? The television? Did you put the window alarms on at the back?'

And I who know very well I did all of those things, start to panic and say, 'I don't know! I don't know!'

So he sighs and growls and we have to go and unlock the front door and check everything again. I think most people are like this, aren't they? In this more security-conscious era? It only makes sense.

Well, then we are standing at our front door, having whizzed round the house and checked everything again, when next door's front door opens and I'm expecting to see one of the Fosters stepping out. I brace myself to say a bright and breezy 'good morning', though I'm certain to be rebuffed. But the words freeze in my throat.

Two young teenagers are stepping out into the front garden of Number 72. They are obviously twins. A boy and a girl. Pretty little things with blonde hair and stripy t-shirts. They aren't saying anything to each other. They don't even notice me, gawping at them, over the hedge.

I watch them move off, almost uncertainly, down the shale garden path. My heart goes out to the pair of them. Whether because they have the misfortune to be related to the Fosters, or whether it is because they seem so uncertain and timid, I don't know. Certainly, they are going off down the street, holding hands, looking as if this place is a very strange and bewildering one. They also look like very old-fashioned children to me. Their clothes, for instance, are unlike any you'd see worn by the other kids round here.

Robert doesn't see them at all and is reliant on my inadequate description of their oddness, once we are in the car and heading towards the ring road and the motorway north.

'I don't see what's so odd about it,' he pronounces. 'They'll be their nephew and niece, or something. Or, I don't know, something like that. Look at this idiot! I'll bet that does his ego some good, overtaking me like that.'

I don't like it when Robert begins his very aggressive talk. Especially in the car. He does it at supermarket checkouts too, and I try to move away.

I didn't think those twins were nephew and niece to the Fosters. All weekend in Grasmere I think about it. I'm picturing their little, worried faces in my head as we visit the

Woollens shops and the gingerbread shop and take a picnic lunch up to Tarn How. Robert won't pay café prices, but we enjoy our picnics anyway, though Tarn How's now spoiled by too many people knowing about its 'edenic seclusion', as Robert calls it. I ask if this makes us – me and him – Adam and Eve. He just starts taking photos of rocks and trees. I sigh because he never takes any with people in. 'What people, eh?' he always laughs. 'What people do we know that we'd want pictures of?'

If I'd been holding his camera when I was on our doorstep, and he was fiddling with the complicated alarm system, I'd have snapped a quick piccie of those twins. Then I could have shown him what I meant about them not being right somehow. It was something in their eyes. Like they were out of their element.

For the next few weeks I think Robert was getting sick of me. Going on and on about it. I think I probably got obsessed with goings-on next door.

'For god's sake woman,' he would say, when I grew distracted over dinner. We were eating in the kitchen and I could hear noises through the thin partition wall. 'Leave them be. They've obviously got visitors again.'

How could he look so unruffled by it? How come he wasn't bothered?

But he was going through a rough time at work just then. They had brought in new systems for everything and he was finding it difficult to deal with. A new spirit of *openness* and *transparency* had come in, he said, when he tried to explain it to me once. Of course I don't really understand these things, but I try my best to be supportive.

He was right that I was getting obsessed, though. I saw more children coming and going at Number 72, next door. More and more of them. All ages, all types. Fat and small, tall and ginger, black and Chinese. All dressed badly, like out of a charity shop. Some of them laughing and running, others lethargic and anxious. The Fosters' home was overrun with them, it seemed.

In our own, rather quiet home, we would hear the staircase next door thudding and thundering as kids ran up and down. The old floorboards would quake beneath all that boistrous energy. At night you could hear Mr Foster yelling at them, to make them quieten down. Once, I even heard Mrs Foster sing a lullaby. I was sitting on the toilet and I heard this whispering, wobbling voice on the other side of the wall. It gave me a turn.

Another time I woke in the night, seized with fear. Cries had rung out. Really horrible screams and then sobbing. The heart-stopping sound of a child in distress. I sat bolt upright in our bed and found that Robert was already awake. I switched on my light. His expression was grim. 'I hate to say it. But I think you're right about something going on next door.'

And even though I was scared for the kids still, my heart glowed at his words.

Yet we didn't do anything. Morning and clarity and sunlight came and, over his toast and his paper, Robert said, 'I think they are probably fostering these children. I have thought it over and of course that's what they're doing. The Fosters are foster parents.' He smiled and returned to the *Daily Mail*.

I sank the plunger of the cafétière with unusual force. I didn't want to go on about it, but I knew he was wrong. I waved him off to his job, to face another day of *openness* and *transparency* and I tried to think about it logically. Surely the Fosters were too old for fostering or adopting. Social Services would never let them start up, this late in life, would they? They would never pass the checks. He looked like a wife-beater. But what did I know? I was tempted to phone Social Services myself. Ask some questions about all these kids, coming and going.

You hear such things, don't you? You read about terrible things. And it's under the noses of ordinary people like us that they go on. And sometimes people turn a blind eye. That's how kids get whisked away and abducted. Held underground for years and tortured. Or piled into lorries, hundreds at a time and dragged to foreign countries. That's what goes on these days. That's what they reckon.

I was having my coffee, watching the *Trisha* show and letting my mind rove over the quandry. Was I looking for sinister things when there was nothing sinister to find?

'You should get out more,' Robert had started to tell me. 'Get yourself a little job. On the tills at Marks and Spencers or something. See some life, Helen. This is no good. Stewing indoors and letting your ideas go mad.'

I took myself off down the high street. I had to pop in the bank and pick up a few things. I was just on Albert Road, before the railway bridge, when I saw Mr Foster coming towards me. I would have to pass him. It would look odd if I crossed the road now. And I was sure he would see all the suspicion plain on my face.

He wasn't alone, either. He had a little girl with him. She must have been about four. Eating a bag of sweets and wearing a knitted cardigan. As they approached Mr Foster reached down and took hold of her hand. For the first time ever, he addressed me directly: 'Good morning, Mrs Booth.'

I returned this greeting, smiling down at the little girl. 'She's lovely. What's her name?'

'Jemima. She's staying with us for a short while. She's my wife's sister's grandchild.'

I was bending awkwardly, trying to say hello to the child. I've never been any use with them. I don't think children take me at all seriously. When I spoke the child looked up and I gave a small gasp of fright, which I tried to stifle. One of Jemima's eyes was half-closed and you could see there was only darkness behind it. The other eye was wide, bright and blue. Surely they could have her wear a patch or something?

Mr Foster had obviously noticed my flinching attempt to cover up my reaction. He looked disgusted and swept away with the child, giving me a curt goodbye.

I was left feeling miserable, like I had failed some test, or been purposefully cruel. I felt even more like that when I told Robert, that evening.

'How could you recoil from a child? She'll remember that. She'll be traumatised.'

'Nonsense,' I said, knitting. In order to make myself feel better, I'd been to the wool shop on the high street. I was making a jumper for the little girl. It had been a long time since I'd knitted anything, and concentrating was making me cross.

'They can't all be great-nephews and nieces, though,' Robert mused, as my needles clacked away. We were watching *Question Time*, which always gets him happily riled up, and shouting at the screen. I was glad that his mind was still running on the problem of next door.

But he didn't say anything more about it until the weekend.

Saturday morning he was out digging the borders. He was happy in old cords and a favourite jumper, seeing to his garden. It was a beautiful morning. I was surprised the kids next door weren't out playing yet. How many were there now, at this point? It gave me an odd feeling, just thinking about it and not knowing how many children were living next door. We had fallen asleep last night, listening to them running up and down the stairs and slamming doors. Mr Foster's voice bellowing at them to quieten down. To settle for the night.

I did the dishes, thinking back over this, enjoying the hot suds and the squeaky clean crockery, and the sunlight on my face. I was only half-aware of watching my husband, digging up the flower beds by the fence we shared with next door. I know the wooden boards there were loose and unsatisfactory. I know that he had been meaning to talk with the Fosters about clubbing together to buy a new fence. As I watched now, I saw him put his spade through the crumbling, mildewy wood. I heard him swear loudly. And then I saw him bend to look at what he'd dug up. And I saw him jump backwards in alarm.

I had never seen him like that. He came into the kitchen shaking like a leaf. I tried to hold him, to offer him hot sweet tea, but he shook me off. 'Come and see, Helen,' he said, though, given his reaction, I wasn't at all keen. I followed him out the back door, across the patio and onto the lawn and I'd have given anything to turn around and go back indoors.

'There,' he said, prising back the boards and the heaped, black earth. 'I thought it was an old tree root, or something. Caught underneath the fence. But look! Look at it, Helen!'

It was a child's arm. White and covered in crumbly black mud. Its hand and splayed fingers seemed curiously expressive to me. I looked at them, rather than at the bloody stump at the other end of the arm.

We sat in the front room to wait for the police. I made that sugary tea at last and we sat huddled together, on dining room chairs, drinking it quickly. I gave myself hiccups, of course, and sat there, like a fool, hiccupping.

'They're killing them,' Robert said, at last.

I shushed him, and hiccupped.

'They're hacking them up and burying them in their garden. Why didn't we know? How come we couldn't tell?'

I didn't say anything. But I'd known something was wrong. I'd known something was going on, all that time. I didn't point that out now.

'They're killers, Helen. Like Fred and Rose West. That's what they are.'

We sat waiting, feeling useless. Too scared to move or do anything else. All the while we knew that the Fosters were home next door, and they had kids in there with them. It was a normal Saturday morning, unseasonably sunny. They weren't to know yet that their game was up. Their happy family business of child mutilation was over now. We were about to put a stop to it.

The police came round much faster than they had for our burglary, back in March. They shot round like I don't know what. 'Body parts' seem to be the magic words for emergency calls. 'Child's body parts' even more so. Three cars came. The police came traipsing into our house looking very serious indeed and I could have died of relief at the sight of them. Something about the uniforms makes me feel instantly guilty, though. I wanted to shout and protest: 'It wasn't us! We're the good people! It was them next door!'

But the police were impartial, professional. They asked to be led to this grisly find in the flower bed. 'Yes, of course,' said my husband, much cooler and calmer than I knew he felt.

I watched from the back door. Robert and five uniformed coppers clustered round the overturned earth. They stood there for some moments, staring at the ground.

Something was wrong.

'It was there! We both saw it!' Robert sounded desperate, even to me. 'It was an arm! A severed child's arm!'

They talked to him in low, warning voices for some minutes. Then they came marching back through our house, muttering threatening things about our wasting police time.

Then the police were gone.

'A dog must have had it,' Robert said, ashen-faced. 'Or...'

Or... I think I knew what he was about to say. Or, next door had somehow whizzed out and removed the evidence before the police got here. That's what they had done. They had watched us out there. They had seen us staring at the arm. And, when our backs were turned, one of them had dashed out and grabbed it. Leaving just an innocent hole in the ground. And making the two of us look sick in the head.

Bang. Bang bang. It was our front door again, shattering the tense quiet of our post mortem. I went to answer it.

There was a little boy there, in grey shorts and a white t-shirt. Funny-looking little thing. 'I've been sent round to ask what the coppers were out for,' he said, in a gruff voice. 'Is something the matter?'

'Erm,' I said. 'No, there isn't. False alarm.'

He rubbed his nose on the back of his hand. 'OK, then.'

I stopped him. 'Do you live next door?'

He nodded. 'Yep.'

'Where did you come from? Are you related to the Fosters?'

He stared at me like I was talking nonsense. He shrugged. Then he thrust a scrappy piece of paper into my hand, turned abruptly and ran off, back down our path, and up next door's. He slammed their door behind him, as if it was the world outside that wasn't safe.

'What did he give you?' Robert asked over my shoulder.

I unfolded the note. It was from Mrs Foster. Requesting the pleasure of our company. Drinks this evening, round theirs. Oh god.

Mrs Foster was a different person at home.

The rooms were busy and crowded with chintz and vulgar ornamentation. Robert tried to catch my eye a number of times as we gazed around at her horrendous collection of unicorns, gonks, china baby dolls. But I feel guilty for looking down on other people's taste, even at the best of times. An old Charlotte Church CD was playing. Back from when she had the voice of an angel. And there was Mrs Foster, tipsy and welcoming in a spangly top, offering us drinks and saying: 'We've meant to have you round so many times. We never got round to it, we've been so remiss, and you were so good to us that Christmas. You haven't met any of our children, have you? Not properly?'

And there they all were. The house seemed to be filled with them. There was no sign of Mr Foster yet, and his wife was like the old woman who lived in a shoe. There were pre-teens sprawled on the armchairs and settee in the living room, quietly watching cartoons. Leggy, ungainly teenagers – the twins I had seen first of all, the day we went to the Lakes – were laying out a buffet on the dining table sideboard. There was a grapefruit with sausage and pineapple cocktail things stuck in it. 'They're all very keen to meet the neighbours,' Mrs Foster beamed at us. 'And it was the kids who did all the eats. They insisted on doing it all themselves.'

That made me shiver, the way she said 'eats'. There was such relish to everything she said. It turned my stomach, as did the sight of the devilled eggs and the stuffed tomatoes. Everything in that place was slightly too colourful. And moist. Everything was glistening.

Robert was polite and inscrutable. 'We had no idea you and Mr Foster had such a large family.'

She smiled. 'Ah yes. None of our very own. But our relatives always seem to need us for baby-sitting and so on.' She was hugging the little boy who had brought our invitation. He was squirming playfully in her grasp.

We knew this couldn't be right. There was never any sign of other adults pulling up in their cars, dropping children off. Didn't she have any better explanation?

The teenaged children were looking at us, and waiting for us to serve ourselves from their buffet. As we shuffled along, inspecting all the dishes and dutifully loading up our paper plates, they were acting like waiting staff. They passed us napkins and smiled at our choices. I could sense Robert growing more and more perturbed.

Mr Foster was in the kitchen, wiping his large hands on a tea towel. He, at least, was his usual self: unwelcoming and gruff. He stared at us. He looked us up and down. 'It's very good of you to invite us,' I said.

'Unexploded bomb was it?' he said sharply. 'Is that what hubby found? Is that why you had the police out?'

'Actually, no,' Robert said.

I looked at him, and he was flushing with colour. I dreaded him telling this man what he had seen.

'It was nothing like that.' But he didn't explain himself any further.

Then, a very pretty girl of about nineteen came swishing past in a nylon blouse, to fetch a vast bottle of Tizer from the fridge. The mood in the kitchen dissipated and I returned to the sitting room, where Mrs Foster breathlessly introduced me to the children.

I was glad to see Jemima again, the girl with the dark hole where her eye should be. This time I made a point of smiling, and not flinching when she looked up at me. As Mrs Foster called out the rest of the names I had a crazy, fleeting moment of feeling like I was in *The Sound of Music*.

We sat there for about half an hour. Small talk. Smiling and sipping. Mrs Foster telling me bits and pieces about the kids in her care. She loved them, I decided. Now I could see how much she cared for them.

'Would you like one, Mrs Booth?' Mrs Foster asked at last, with such a shy, sidelong smile. 'Wouldn't you just love to pick one up and take it home?'

And, without thinking, I said: 'Yes. Yes, of course I would.'

Then we were interrupted.

Robert was telling me: 'Helen. Helen. Time for home.'

At the door Mr Foster himself waved us off. Out of hearing of his wife, and under the pretext of explaining to Robert how he'd repaired their garden gate, he hissed: 'Keep well out of it. You and your wife. We don't like it, the way you look at us. You're looking at our kids. They've noticed you doing it. You want to watch out. You don't want to worry kiddies like that with your inappropriate attention. Do you?'

Robert stiffened and I caught my breath. Neither of us said anything. We were too shocked to say anything back to him. What did he think he was accusing us of? We couldn't believe it. He snorted at us and turned away, and went back up his pathway, crunching the blue slate chippings under his carpet slippers. Some of the kids were in the doorway, watching us, and Mrs Foster was already back indoors. Their door slammed abruptly and me and Robert were left out in the street, quite stunned.

'I don't like this,' he said.

'The kids seem happy, well-cared for,' I said.

'Hm.' He unlocked our door. Three locks at the front, we've got.

'Did we hallucinate it?' I said as I switched on the lamp in the hall, and he grappled with the alarm system. 'The arm, I mean. Did we really see it?'

'Of course we saw it, Helen. It was a human arm. A child's arm.'

By now I wasn't sure anymore. I was still thinking about Mrs Foster perched next to me, telling me all about the kids in her charge. She had been so close in that sitting room, as I picked at the chicken satay, I could smell the brandy on her breath, all sickly. I had braved myself to ask about Jemima.

'What happened to her eye?'

'Her eye? Oh. She came to us in that state. Bless her little heart.'

That sentence kept coming back into my head as I lay

awake in our bedroom at the back of the house, the moonlight glaring down on us. Robert tends to sleep easily, deeply, like a flat fish sunk at the bottom of the sea. I'm roving over everything, my eyes frantic and staring at the ceiling. That's how I spend my nights, with fears and fretfulness mounting up in my brain. And that night I was thinking about Mrs Foster going: 'She came to us in that state.' Like Jemima was faulty goods.

I drifted off to sleep for maybe twenty minutes. These days, since our break-in, I've found it quite hard. I'm awake at every little squeak and groan from outside. What wakes me up this time is noise out in the gardens. And it's not that sinister, almost noiseless-noise of burglars creeping about and trying so hard to be silent. It's not that. I can hear squeals and whoops. I can hear children's voices, inarticulate with excitement. Lots of them.

It's like Christmas out there in the stark moonlight. What's going on? My heart hammers so hard I can't think rationally. I elbow Robert hard and he shifts and doesn't wake. Are they laughing out there? Are they screaming? I have this vision of them all running out of the house, escaping from the Fosters' clutches. I struggle to the window and get tangled in the endless net curtains. I squint and I struggle to see.

There, down below, neatly plotted and hemmed with hedges, trees and fences, our gardens are laid out and still. All except for the Fosters' garden, where there's something like fifteen children, of all ages, hopping about on the lawn. They are shouting and jostling and some of them are dashing around for what looks like the sheer fun of it. Even though I'm scared and confused, the sight of them makes me want to laugh. 'Robert!' I hiss. 'Wake up! Come here!'

And then I see that Mr and Mrs Foster are out there as well. I look at the digital clock and it's past 4am. All of the foster children, and the Fosters themselves are still dressed for the day. Mrs Foster is just as silly and excited as the kids. She joins hands with some of the younger ones. They're dancing ring-a-rosy on the wet lawn.

Mr Foster has fetched a garden fork.

'You're missing it, Robert! Come and see!'

From the depths of the duvet, which he has wound about him, as per usual, like giant human kitchen roll, Robert groans and swears at me. I don't call him again. I can't. I'm watching Mr Foster as he carries his garden fork across the lawn. He moves through the milling children and the moonlight glints off the sharp fork tines.

How could we have thought anything was amiss? They all look so happy. They all look glad to be alive. They are jumping about and flexing their fresh young limbs. They're springing about on the damp lawn. Suddenly I realise I would do anything to be with them. To be part of that family party. That atmosphere they somehow live in. And yet I feel so distant. Peering round my net curtains, up here. Left out of it all.

And here is Mr Foster, digging in his cabbage patch. Gardening at weird times in the night. Well, they're eccentric, aren't they? We know that by now.

'Wouldn't you love to pick one up and just take it home?' That's what Mrs Foster asked me. And she knew she was striking some deep-rooted chord within me. It chimed out loud inside my chest and it was chiming now, as I watched them all dancing and playing. Of course I would. Of course I would love one of my own. If they had one to spare.

Weird thoughts to have in the middle of the night. Weird thoughts to have, any time of day. No matter how muddled you are, or jarred, or scared.

I'm watching Mr Foster in his vegetable garden as he loosens the roots beneath his cabbages. Delicate, so delicate, the way he works. Some of the children gather to watch. They coo and applaud. And over comes Mrs Foster, swaying on her tiny feet and kicking up the shining dew. She bends to kneel before one particular cabbage. She brushes the damp soil from its outer leaves. Mr Foster has cut it free and he steps back, looking satisfied. The children whoop and cry and he shushes them quickly. This is all supposed to be secret. What would happen if they woke some nosey parker, eh? This is a special treat, their being let out here tonight. Never again, though. They are far too noisy. They are naughty children and they will never be asked again to come outside and witness this. The children fall silent and morose at Mr Foster's stern words. Perhaps he doesn't really mean it.

For now, though, their attention is fixed on Mrs Foster. So is Mr Foster's, and he looks proud. My attention, too, is taken up by the beaming face of Mrs Foster, as she bends to heft the fat cabbage out of its mucky bed. First she pushes her face gently into its leaves and kisses it on the nose.

And then she pulls it free.

The children all cheer and Mr Foster tries to stop them. Then it's a free-for-all, as he gives in and lets them rootle through the leafy rows, searching out hands, feet, ears and whatever else might be growing there.

A Fresh Pair of Eyes

LAVINIA MURRAY

'Where does all the water come from?' the receptionist said, inclining her bobbed head towards a novelty umbrella stand. It was shaped like a large pair of mangled spectacles. Dribbling umbrellas protruded from half the shattered frame, and water pooled on the one undamaged concave lens. The whole thing suggested a grotesquely magnified crime scene. 'That rain's not stopped since you arrived,' the receptionist said. I nodded and gave her a smile that didn't show my teeth. The receptionist continued to regard me. It was as though she had spoken in code and hoped I was the one whose reply would free her of a secret. So I nodded again to let her know I couldn't take her secret, and she turned away, shoulders visibly sagging. My right eye had just been lasered back to its birthright of perfect vision and was still in a state of tender incredulity. Burned by the miraculous, it was so viscously aware of its fragile contents it felt pregnant. My left eye, however, rested smugly in its socket, a veteran of laser surgery. If there were anything to see, left eye would dole out glances the way a slaughterman might pat livestock. I went over to the window. My right eye looked out on a Manchester as solid as compacted sand. Crowds jostled against its crumbling edges, essentially smoothing and mending it. Meanwhile, my left eye caught a large shape slamming into the glass, the impact leaving a greasy, fluid stain. The thing had been spinning like wound rope, or maybe flapping, yet something about it had seemed intrinsically human.

'You're free to go now, ' the receptionist said, jolted out of reverie by the sudden bang but with no interest in what might have caused it. I had rested for the obligatory thirty minutes in the recovery lounge with its quiet décor, subdued lighting, and violent sounds, noises caused by an aquarium that had air sprayed into it like buckshot at close range, and a water cooler where every cup that drained from it hurled gas through its belly like a grenade. I retrieved my coat and watched new patients entering through the rotating doors. Reaching the polished wood and chrome desk they suddenly became conscious of their faulty eyes. They blinked rapidly, removed and polished their glasses, and studied the message of the umbrella stand. Then they stared as though their eyelids were already immobilised by elegant clamps and filigree scaffolding, feeling the silver wing nuts tightening until each eyeball was naked and friendless. I smiled reassuringly, slipped my bag over my arm, and stepped out onto the street. It was as if I had just completed a school detention, not a life-changing medical procedure.

The rain had stopped and the wind had risen, shaking droplets from the unlit Christmas lights strung between buildings. Overhead, a full moon gouged through clouds like a nut cracking open its own shell. That's when something changed. Now, my education declares that the brain is an organ of biased interpretation, running a faulty retrieval system, prone to abuse by deductive reasoning and accumulative superstition. It is supposed to deliver, on an admittedly ad hoc basis, opinions into the conscious mind, and twisted uncertainty into dreams, What it had offered, up to that moment, was always within the narrow parameters of possibility, fed a thin diet by severely short-sighted eyes. And here I was, on the threshold of perfect vision with a sense of unease. What could I see? What would become visible? I hurried along Deansgate, turned up Portland Street and crossed into Albert Square. As the town hall clock struck six I could see people erratically circling the statues, driven and directed by the more purposeful pedestrians crossing the square. Several of these aimless people were suffering from horrifically deformed feet, their flesh bunched and swollen, leaning out of misshapen shoes. Strands of twine cut across their ankles as they limped, frequently stopping to rest on their least damaged leg. One of the obviously healthier males was tagged, his left trouser cuff gripped by a numbered band. What felony had he committed? Surely a white collar crime? He had the bearing of a barrister, so he must have succumbed to perjury or fraud. Yes, fraud or road rage, and he'd drive an S.U.V. or something intimidating, sporty and personalized. He suddenly spotted a ragged group congregating around a young couple seated on a bench eating cake and drinking coffee, and he scurried to join them. These oddly meandering people were angling towards dropped crumbs, losing their nerve at the last moment and continuing past the couple, who hadn't noticed them. Then it struck me. I was watching human pigeons. My arm rose and my finger pointed. I shook. Someone else needed to witness what I was seeing, so I dragged at the first sleeve that brushed against me. I turned to face the person I had detained. It was the barrister pigeon. I'd startled him, his hard, toothless mouth was open with shock, and he fluttered and worked himself free of my grasp. Then he leapt into the air, skimming the ground for twenty metres before coming to rest and resuming his search for food. Several of the bolder pigeon people had wandered over to me and were now making sideways passes, their heads angled enquiringly. I showed them my empty hands. 'No food.' I said gently, 'I've nothing for you. I'm sorry.' and they wandered away, only one young female giving me an admonishing backward glance. Such round orange eyes in human faces, I thought! Such rigidly pursed lips and weak, reclining chins! And in such large numbers — there must have been sixty or seventy of them gathered there.

I left the square. I had to do something. I ran down Cross Street and bought two carrier bags full of sandwiches, literally emptying the shelves of stock. As I left the shop, one of the pigeon people, an elderly woman, unshod and with stumps for feet, hobbled past.

'Excuse me, are you hungry?' I called after her, but she leapt across the street and disappeared. Where she headed? Where else would the pigeon people go? I knew I had to gauge how big a population there was, how large the problem might be. So I walked towards Victoria Station, scanning the street, cutting down by the sparsely lit cathedral gardens. There I managed to corner one, a little, feeble boy in soiled sportswear. He smelled, and his lank hair was glued to the wet scabs covering his neck. He also had a racking cough. I offered him a sandwich. 'Don't be frightened. Please take it. You look starved.' But he trembled and backed away, his eyes darting about as he sought a way past me. That's when a hundred others fell out of nowhere, dripping from the darkness, knocking the bags from my hands. Then, as a mass, they all bent double and began working at the sandwiches, throwing them a little way into the air, and feverishly attacking the rigid packaging with their lips. Several packs came open and fights broke out as the strongest claimed them and ate, their fists balled, arms raised, ready to punch.

I have just walked away from them. I do not understand what they are. Do they have a purpose? Now I know they exist, am I morally obliged to feed them? Or shall I inform the authorities who I know regularly undertake culls?

Tight Wrappers

CONRAD WILLIAMS

Mantle stopped a taxi on the Edgware Road and piled in. He was breathless and, as always, a little panicky that he'd dropped something, that he was missing some essential part.

'Holland Park,' he said, patting the pockets of his raincoat. The hand of another pedestrian, cheated by Mantle's claiming of the cab, slapped against the back window as the taxi moved off, leaving behind an imprint that took some time to fade.

Mantle had stolen the coat from a theme park staffroom a couple of decades previously, attracted by the numerous deep pockets, the better for storing his lists, address books, notes and clippings, his maps, an urban *disjecta membra*, the city in leaves. At times he felt as though he were a disorganised filing cabinet on the lam. Occasionally he fell asleep on his bed in his coat. He felt naked without it, or more specifically, that special form of insulation that his papers provided.

The day was a blur in his thoughts, as most were. He struggled to remember what he had breakfasted on, only that it had been in a coffee shop on Old Compton Street, half an eye on the newspaper, his notebook with its codes and descants, the phone in his fist. He had gone on to sell a couple of Fine/Fine Iain Sinclairs, doubles from his own collection, in a sandwich shop at the north side of Blackfriars Bridge before scuttling along the Jubilee Walkway to the National Film Theatre where he met Rob Swaines, his 'Southwark

Mole'. Over the years Rob had fed him some great information on the underground book networks of SE1. He had learned of a Graham Greene first, sitting forgotten in a plastic washtub of an Oxfam in Stamford Street, an early Philip K Dick in a Fitzalan Street squat, a news vendor by the tube station at Lambeth North carried in his pocket a copy of HG Wells' *The Island of Dr Moreau* containing an inscription to its recipient from the author not to read it at night.

The rest of the day was a smear of motion, of buses caught at full pelt, of observations written in the corner of a fried chicken cesspit, of phone calls, hot and cold leads, rumours of a Bradbury unclipped, *Dark Carnival*, in a Battersea pub that came to nothing, hastily scribbled ideas for a book hunt in Edinburgh, catching up with the tracings of his route on the OS maps, marginalia he had forgotten about but that, freshly discovered, sparked more calls, more possibilities; there was no such thing as a closed door in London, he had learned. Every shelf was a display for him; it was just a matter of time before he got round to cherry-picking the best of the best from each one.

He'd received a text from Heaton, his main bloodhound, his *in*, not five minutes previously, alerting him to a rare Very Good/Good in W8. It was pleasing that he was already in the area; if the traffic favoured him he could be on Aubrey Road within minutes. He pulled out his battered Moleskine and slipped off the elastic binding. Inside he flipped through alphabeticised jottings, references to books he had in his sights, rare tomes, the jackets of which he sometimes felt under his fingertips in the moments before he became fully awake. Here was his file on Mick Bett, the thriller writer whose first two novels, *Black Iris* and *One Man On His Own*, published in the early 1960s, had been turned into quirky cult films starring George Kennedy. Bett had killed himself in 1967 when he had become blocked on his third novel, working title *The Mummer*, at a time when the

James Bond franchise had hit its stride and a year after Adam Hall's first Quiller novel, *The Berlin Memorandum*, had been turned into a successful film. Mantle wondered if the Sunday Times encomium on the front cover of the Pan paperback of *One Man On His Own* ("The best, after Deighton and Le Carré") might have contributed to Bett's decision to leap from the Golden Gate Bridge.

Mantle owned a signed first edition, first printing of *Black Iris* that he had bought at a Brighton book fair in 1976 for a wallet-bruising thirty pounds. The very same book was now worth seven thousand pounds. Mantle's assessment of a book's future worth was rarely off the mark. He had no compunction about spending a lot for a Fine/Fine now if his hunch whispered that there'd be a few more noughts on its value a decade hence. Heaton's digging had led to this evening's revelation; a copy of *OMOHO* sitting on a shelf in west London, its spine having probably never known any strain.

The traffic was snarled around Marble Arch; Mantle felt blisters of sweat rise on his forehead. He couldn't relax despite the knowledge that the book, having occupied its place on the Aubrey Road shelf for the last twenty years, wasn't going anywhere in the next ten minutes. His gaze was snagged on a criss-cross of scaffolding clinging to the face of an Edwardian house facing Hyde Park. Light snaked along the tubes and died on the dirty orange plastic netting. The house seemed diminished by the complexity, the aggressive sprawl of the construction. Scaffolding bothered him, it pulled at his vision like a scar.

'What are you reading?' Mantle asked the driver as he shoved the notebook back into its nest. A thriller-fat paperback rested open-bellied on the dashboard. Mantle had learned to quell his disgust at the way other people treated their reading matter, forced into supine positions they did not deserve.

'That Dan Brown guy,' the driver said, eventually, predictably. Mantle could dismiss him now. Him and his Very Poor, his Reading Copy. But it was something he had to know. He had to know what was on the cover, what was being sucked up into the eyes. On the tube he would crick his neck to catch a glimpse of any title. He was about to return to his notes, to trace the latest leg of his years-long journey through the capital on his OS map, when the driver came back with a question of his own.

'No,' Mantle said, trying to keep the edge from his voice. 'I've never read *The Da Vinci Code*. It's... not my thing.'

He'd been offered a signed Mint in April, but he wouldn't have forgiven himself, could never have allowed it to rub shoulders with his Lovecrafts and Priests, his M.R.s and his M. Johns. It was snobbery, to be sure, but the very act of collecting, serious collecting, was snobbery anyway. Mantle was too old, too alone to care what anybody thought of him or his obsession. All that mattered to him were the pencil webs he spun across his map of London, the treasure he was tracking from Shepherd's Bush to Shoreditch.

The taxi disgorged him on the corner of Aubrey Road. A light rain, so insubstantial as to be barely felt, breathed against him. He looked back at the Bayswater Road and saw it ghosting across the harsh sodium lighting like the sheets of cellophane he wrapped around the jackets of his hardbacks, to further protect them. He darted away from the main drag, patting his pockets, fretting over the corners of reminders, receipts, appointments, all the clues that frothed dangerously at the lips of his pockets.

He found the address he needed and rapped hard on the front door. He smoothed down his hair and hoped the occupants wouldn't be able to smell his odour, a mix of stale sweat and old paper, not really that bad, but perhaps offensive to those who were not used to it.

A well-dressed woman with professionally styled hair answered the door. She was in her late-fifties, it seemed to Mantle, although the way she was turned out made her appear quite a bit younger. Her expression was cold; she was chewing something, a chicken leg, nub of white gristle gleaming, clutched in her hand. He cursed himself. She had been drawn from dinner. She wanted him gone; no amount of charm would work now.

'I apologise for disturbing your dinner,' he said.

'Quite all right,' she snapped. 'What is it?'

'A book.'

'A book?' Now her expression did change, to one of bafflement.

'My name's Henry Mantle. I'm a collector, a diviner of text. I've got friends call me Sniffer.'

'You've got friends,' she said.

Mantle's smile faltered as he wondered if she were belittling him, but he pressed on. 'Anyway, I understand you have a copy of Mick Bett's novel, *One Man On His Own*, published in 1962. I'd like to make you an offer for it.'

A further change. The woman, consciously or not, closed the door a fraction. 'How did you know I had that?'

'A receipt in a ledger in a Bloomsbury hotel. A book fair in the '80s. A purchase traced to you.'

'But this is… this is invasive,' she said.

'Not at all, Mrs Greville,' he said. 'I can assure —'

'How do you know my name?' Needle in the voice now. An aspect of threat.

'The receipt. The book fair.'

'I'm sorry, but I don't like this. Please leave.'

She was making to shut the door and in his desperation he shot out his hand to block it.

'I'll give you twelve hundred pounds,' he said. 'In cash, right now, if you say yes.'

She paused, just as it seemed her anger would overflow

and she would start shouting. The breath seemed knocked from her. Mantle refrained from smiling; he knew he had won.

'Twelve hundred? For a *book*?'

'I'm a big fan of his work. And copies – nice, well-looked after copies – are scarce.'

She seemed to change her mind about him. Maybe she was thinking of all the other unread copies of books on her shelves, perhaps the result of buying sprees by a dearly departed, or something inherited that she couldn't be bothered to take to the charity shop. She drew the door open wider and ushered him in, insisting sharply that he could have five minutes of her time, no more.

He barely took any notice of the hallway he was walking along; the smell of books was in his nostrils. He patted his pockets, felt the comforting scrunch of bus tickets, pencilled symbols and hints, directions and directives etched on paper napkins, beer coasters, cigarette packets. His whole life was in these pockets; he couldn't bear to throw anything away. He supposed it described a weakness in him, a form of psychosis, but he was helpless. He felt emboldened by these layers, these graphite and ink ley-lines. His wallet was fat underneath all of this. He ached for something to happen.

She introduced him to a room whose darkness was penetrated only by a soft, low lozenge of orange light; a cat was curled around the base of the lamp, glancing up unimpressed at Mrs Greville's guest.

'Here's the book,' she said, reaching up to tip a volume into her left palm.

He winced as she handled the book. She wouldn't pass it to him quickly enough, and kept hold of it, turning it around in her fingers as if searching for some clue as to why it was worth what he had offered. She gave him a look; her tongue worked at some shred from her rapidly cooling and forgotten dinner.

'You know, this was my husband's, my late husband's, favourite novel. I really don't think I would feel happy letting it go. It's become something to remember him by.'

Mantle smiled. He had prepared himself for this. It always happened. 'I fully understand. I'm willing to go to sixteen hundred. Which is way over the odds for a book of this sort.'

He could see her scrutinising him, wondering if she could wring out another hundred, wondering how to play the game. But she didn't know anything. She was sold.

'I suppose there's no point in hanging on to the past,' she said. 'My Eddie would want his books to be appreciated by readers rather than gather dust on the shelf.'

Mantle pursed his lips. His mobile phone went off, vibrating against his leg.

'Then you'll take the sixteen hundred?'

'I will,' said Mrs Greville, in a voice of almost comical reluctance.

She passed him the book once the bills were in her hand. He was hastily wishing her good night, wrapping the book in a brown paper bag after a swift, expert appraisal of its jacket, boards and copyright page. 'Very fine, very fine,' he said, his little joke, his signature.

He barely heard Mrs Greville asking if there was anything else he'd like to look at. He fumbled the phone from his pocket and barked his name before the answering service could kick in.

There was no reply, just the sound of air rushing down the line, as if the caller had contacted him from a tunnel, or a windswept beach. There was a pulse to the wind; he was put in mind of the white noise of shortwave signals on his old radio.

'Hello?' he said, his voice thick in his throat. He heard the faint echo of his own greeting, that occasional anomaly of mobile phones. It sounded as though, for a second, he was talking to himself. He might as well have been; nobody replied.

That radio. He wondered where it was now. It had been his father's, but Mantle had spent more time than he twisting its knobs and dials. He would zone in on the pulses and bleats of what he had believed were signals of intent from distant aliens, try to decipher their insistent tattoo. A few months later, after the violent death of his father, he believed they were the frantic, distorted echoes of his last breaths; scorched, impatient, encoded with a meaning he could not extract.

His father had worked as a builder's mate, hod-carrying, mixing cement, making the bacon butty runs. One night he had met a girl in a pub and smuggled her into the site after closing time. Mantle had dramatized what might have happened on many occasions, running sequences and dialogue through his mind like a writer planning a passage in a novel. There were never any happy endings.

He lights cigarettes for them; she tastes the sticky residue of whisky and Guinness on the filter. She watches him lark around, his steel toe capped boots crunching through glass and plaster; the odd, metallic skitter as he kicks a nail across the floor. In here are great mounds of polythene wrap, packaging for fixtures and fittings, looking to her drink-addled mind like greasy clouds frozen into stillness.

He's opened the windows. Outside, the sky is hard with winter. *Goodbye cruel world* as he lurches into the night. A breath catches in her throat. She rushes to see. *Tricked you. Step into my office.* He's giggly, foolish, reckless. Unlike the man who skulks at home, the taciturn man, incapable of tenderness, of affection. The scaffold bites into the building's face like an insect, all folded, fuddled legs. His steps shush and clump on the wood. The angles of metal look cold enough to burn. *Come inside*, she says. She's nervous. This is an unknown, unknowable world to her. It's a sketch of a home. There is no comfort here. She unbuttons her blouse, lets him see the acid white bra, the curve of what it contains. *Come inside.*

Fumbling. Stumbling. An accident. A flame from a match, from the smouldering coals of the cigarettes. A fire leaps, too swift and strong to stamp out. A drunken attempt. The surge of molten plastic. In the flickering orangedark, before she runs to escape, she sees him twisting in the suffocating layers, wrapping himself in clear, wet heat as it melts through his flesh. His fingers fuse together as he tries to claw it from his face. He stands there, silently beseeching, loops of his own cheeks spinning from his hands. The black fug from burning plastic funnels out of him and he staggers to the window, toppling on to that cold, black edifice.

He sees one now. Like an exoskeleton. A riot of violent shapes. His father had never been a great reader, unless you counted *The Sun*, which was never off his dashboard. He had always snorted his derision whenever he found Mantle leafing through an Ian Serraillier, or a David Line. There was always something else to do, in his opinion, as if reading for its own sake, and reading fiction especially, was a waste of time. The scaffolds were erected – that arcane, mysterious practice – and dismantled. They were the means to deliver repair, but Mantle could not, would not see that in them. Whenever he chanced upon them, he saw only his father cooling on the duckboards, black sheaves lifting from his face.

Bitterly, Mantle closed his phone and assessed the road. He couldn't see any taxis but the bus stop across the way was busy; there'd be a 94 along any moment. He joined the queue and extracted the book from his pocket. He sucked in its brittle breath and traced the tightness of the head, the embossing of the title and author on the front cover. Twice what he'd paid would have still been a modest price. Quickly, before the cold air, or the pollution, or his excitement could have any adverse effect on the pages, he slid it back into the brown bag. Books and brown paper, well, there was a perfect marriage. Yet an increasingly unlikely one, in the bookshops he haunted throughout the capital. Flimsy plastic bags, one molecule thin it seemed, were used to package books these days. He'd talked to some of the booksellers, suggested returning to paper, that the books might sweat under plastic, that they could be damaged, but had only ever received blank looks. He liked the snug way the brown paper folded against, *into* the book it was protecting, as opposed to the slip and slide of the plastic, as if it were trying to shun what it sheathed. It was too much like smothering.

A sudden gust of wind; a smack and clatter in the deep dark behind him. He flinched. Nobody else seemed to notice. He stared again at the scaffolding as it snaked up the face of the church. The light was good enough only to see a treacly gleam trace the geometry of the struts and tubes and platforms. It waxed across the netting, creating the impression of a series of rhomboid mouths opening and closing against the night. Mantle mimicked them.

The bus arrived; he boarded, feeling the air condense at his back as if someone were hurrying to catch the bus before it departed, but when he glanced back there was nobody. The doors cantilevered shut. On his way home he noticed so many houses and shops masked by aluminium that he had to reach up to his own face to check it wasn't similarly encumbered.

Mantle's flat: bookshelves everywhere. He had the spaces above the doors adapted to take C format paperbacks. There was shelving in the bathroom, although he had spent a fortune on air-conditioning to ensure that the steam from the shower and bath were negated to ensure his books remained in pristine condition. The floor was a maze of literary magazines, reviews, photocopies of library archive material, letters from booksellers.

He unwrapped the Bett and placed it next to *Black Iris*. The covers hissed together as if sighing with contentment. A completeness there. A job done. He could imagine Mick Bett himself nodding his appreciation. Here was somebody who cared as much for the decent writer of bestsellers – and there were some around – as the leftfield scribes, the slipstreamers, the miserablists. There were writers he adored who had never sold well when people like Jeffrey Archer, Dan Brown, Martina Cole were coining it. Forget clitfic, or ladlit, this was shitlit. He'd rather stick with an arresting, original writer who deserved greater exposure, a writer who cared about the craft, a writer who lived for it – a Joel Lane, a Christopher Burns, a Rhonda Carrier – than some twunt who could hardly write his or her own name, but whose name was gold because of some other supposed talent.

He drew a bath and pulled a bottle of Magners from the fridge. Food was nothing more than a thought. Already he was considering the following day; Heaton had mentioned possibilities in Crystal Palace: an 1838 Elizabeth B Barrett, 'The Seraphim and Other Poems', with an inscription. You were looking at 2.5K plus for that. He took the drink over to his desk and looked out at the city. Books under every roof. Most of them forgotten, badly looked after, unread. He felt the weight of all his own literature bristling behind him, smelled that all-pervading tang of ancient pages.

Something shimmered under the caul of city light. The reflections of red security lamps crept along the wet scaffolds like something alive, determined. Mantle was suddenly shocked by the mass of spars and supports cluttering the skyline. It seemed as if the whole of London was crippled, in need of Zimmer frames and callipers. The night breathed through it all, a carbonised, gasping ebb and flow. A miserable suck, a terrible fluting. He thought he saw something move through the confusion, shadow dark, intent, clumsy. Before it merged with a deeper blackness, right at the heart of the scaffold, he saw, thought he saw, deceleration, the wrap of a hand around a column, black fingers that did not shift until his eyes watered and he had to look away.

Mantle remembered his bath and stood up sharply, knocking over his drink and bashing his knee into the underside of his desk. His foot skidded on the open pages of a magazine and he went down awkwardly, an arm outstretched to stabilise himself serving only to swipe a cairn of novels to the floor. Pages riffled across his line of sight, a skin of words in which to wrap his pain. They wouldn't leave him alone, even after he had managed to wrestle a way into sleep.

His alarm clock didn't so much bring him out of sleep as rescue him from a desperate conviction that he was about to suffocate. He felt as though he were in the centre of a world of layers, and all of them were trying to iron him flat, as if he were some crease that was spoiling the uniformity of his dreamscape. He found himself wearing a tight jacket that was like a corset, pinning his gut back. The city was similarly constricted; he couldn't see brick or stone for the weight of aluminium, slotted with mathematical precision into every available square metre of space. It caused him to feel sick at his own softness; he felt arbitrary, ill-fitting. The books he was carrying seemed to sense his otherness and kept trying to squirm from his grasp. Pages fluttered. He felt the bright sting of a paper cut in his finger. Blood sizzled across onionskin. He gazed at his hands and saw how the print from the books had transferred to his flesh, a backwards code tattooed on every inch. He was ushered into a series of ever-narrowing streets by faces smudged into nonsense by the speed he was moving at, or the lack of oxygen reaching his brain. A building up ahead stood out because of the presence of an open door, a black oblong of perfection among the confused angles. He was fed through it. Shapes gestured and shrugged and pointed. He was shown a gap in the heights, a section of hammerbeam that had rotted and was being prepared for repair. Ladders and platforms were arranged around the workstation like props in a play.

He was cajoled and prodded up the ladder until he reached the ceiling. He was manhandled into the slot, he screamed as his neck was twisted violently to accommodate the rest of his body. Great cranes positioned at either end of the hammerbeam slowly rotated a mechanised nut, the size of a dinner plate. The two ends of the hammerbeam were incrementally forced together. Pressure built in his body; he felt blood rush to his extremities. He bellowed uncontrollably, a nonsense noise, a plea. He felt bones pulverising, unbearable tensions tearing the shiny tight skin of his suit, his stomach. At the last moment, as breath ceased, he saw himself burst open, everything wet in him raining to the floor. It looked like ink. It looked like a river of words.

Coffee. It burned his lip but he was grateful for anything that reminded him he was still alive. His fingers shook a little as he replaced the cup in its saucer. Heaton's last text was burned into his thoughts, helpfully chasing away the remnants of the dream. He spread out a fan of notes on the table, sucking up the gen on this new quarry. Tucked away in a Stoke Newington studio flat was a Mint/Mint of Bryce Tanner's first novel, *Noble Rot*, published by Faber in 1982. According to Heaton, the studio had been abandoned by the occupant, some failed venture capitalist who had needed a temporary base while he searched for his Hoxton warehouse. Rumour was he'd drowned himself in one of the reservoirs in N16. The flat had been left as it was while his nearest and dearest were sought, a process taking longer than had been expected. Armed with a hammer, Mantle had cased the building an hour previously, and had been encouraged by the lack of humanity;

the building seemed little more than a shell giving the come-on to the wrecking ball and the softstrip crews. The jitters Mantle was suffering on the back of his dream, and a need to be sure of what he was about to do, had driven him away in search of caffeine. Now, sitting on a hard metal chair outside a deli in Church Street, the call of the book was too great to resist any longer. He tossed a handful of coins into his saucer and retraced his steps to the High Street. A block sitting back off that busy main drag contained more boards than glass in its window frames. Mantle negotiated the buckled front door and the inevitable climb up the stairs. Broken glass was scattered across every landing; dead insects provided a variety to the crunch under his shoes. The door he needed was padlocked – cheaply – and his hammer dealt with it after a couple of blows. Inside he paused in case his attack had brought any remaining residents to investigate, but either the building was deserted or apathy reigned. It didn't matter – he wasn't going to be disturbed.

The studio was well maintained, leaning towards minimalism but with enough books, CDs and DVDs to suggest that it was a life choice that wasn't being taken seriously. There was nothing to suggest that its inhabitant was likely to take his own life, but Mantle was no psychologist. He didn't care one jot. All that mattered to him was that couple of pounds of paper and board.

He located the book almost immediately. It seemed to call to him from among all the dog-eared paperbacks. It had presence, gravitas. He slid it clear from the shelf and hefted it reverentially.

The book turned to ash in his fingers.

He stood there for a while, as the air seemed to darken around him, his mouth open, trying to keep himself together. The notes in his pocket lost their insulating properties. He was in a cold room, bare but for a bucket filled with a dried meringue of shit.

The boards across the window had collapsed; wind flooded in. He moved towards it, the flakes in his hand rising up like angered insects. Scaffolding bit deep into the pebbledashed skin of the block. Through the shapes it created he could almost imagine he could see the muscular City architecture, the Gherkin, the old Nat West tower and, further afield, Canary Wharf. The aircraft warning lights they pulsed might shine in the tubing outside this very window, but also, deep within him, matching the insistent thrum of his own heart. He heard the creak of the broken door behind him and he acted upon it, not wanting to turn to see what had followed him up here. Falteringly, he clambered out onto the platform and edged along it until he had reached the end. His hands, coated with the dust of a book he could still smell, clawed at the brackets that kept the entire structure married to the block. They were so cold they scorched his skin.

He heard something struggle out of the window frame and onto the duckboards. Whatever it was had no grace, no balance. Its weight sent stresses and strains along the planks to his own feet, lifting them a little. The song of the wood might have been the keening that played in his throat. He smelled the high, narcotic smell of burned plastic. There were no books. There were no notes. No text messages. No Heaton. No wallet filled with cash. No Mrs Greville. No Mick Bett. No Gherkin. No past, no future. No nothing. Mantle's love of books was desperate, a wish never to be fulfilled. He reached up to his eyes and pressed his fingers against the dry membrane that filmed them. Pockets of interior colour exploded. He could never know what it meant to be able to read a story, no more than he would ever learn what colour his own eyes were.

The lie these books contained. The fictions. It had a face, it had a fury. They infected your life, it was a contagion. You built up your own monster from the deceptions you invented. And Mantle was all about deceit. He turned to confront what had chased him all this way, all these years. Not being able to see him gave Mantle a Pyrrhic victory of sorts. He was able to smile, his mouth finding an unusual cast even as the sum of his trickery leaned in close. The hand over his mouth was little more than crisped talons. He felt as if he were becoming infected by that alien flesh, growing desiccated, so sucked dry of moisture that his face might disintegrate. His chest muscles ruptured with the strain of trying to draw a breath. Millions of capillaries burst, flooding his inner sight with red. He heard the stutter and gargle of his own breath, or of the thing silencing him. White noise. Explosions of crumpled paper. In extremis, he managed to kiss the hand, to reach out and hold tight, to imagine that this was the hug he had craved for so long.

Horror Story

PAUL CORNELL

I enter the building, and there's the black discontinuity for a moment, then the sound of the door closing. Chunk. The room takes a moment to load, the bar on the screen holding back for a moment before giving way, so something's going on in there.

A figure is standing there, looking past me. 'Pickpocket Sofia?' asks the screen. Sofia is a tall girl in a blue dress, with a faux medieval cap and belt. My target indicator shows that Sofia is still unaware of me, so I could strike her with one schlonk of my blade for 6x sneak attack damage.

Instead, I come out of sneak mode and approach Sofia. When I get to a certain distance, she's suddenly looking straight at me and speaking to me, her hand coming up as she sees me. That still scares me when it happens in the street, or in the middle of sleep.

Sofia speaks with one of the two voices they have for women. There are five or so voices for the men. 'Greetings, outlander.' Her expression is kind: she's well-disposed towards me. At least an eighty. But is there something at the edge of that, something about the curl of her mouth? Is she laughing at me rather than with me?

They ought to give these things to autistic kids. I think I mean autistic. The kids who can't understand facial expressions.

I'm given three options as to what I can say. General

topics. 'Henri.' 'Incidents in the Town.' 'Seeking an Appointment with the King.' I hit 'Henri'.

'Henri is in the Citadel,' she says, calmly. Then: 'he has been meddling with things he should not be!' Sudden anger, as if the actor is reacting only to the exclamation mark at the end of the line.

The option continues to glow white. She has more to tell me about Henri, but she doesn't yet trust me enough.

I've been doing this since 10pm the day before yesterday, room time. I seem to have lost the need for water. I haven't pissed, either. I haven't felt the need. My arm's been in basically the same position for all that time, but no pins and needles. This must all be because of them. It's now 3.03 am by the clock radio beside my bed.

Another three hours and they probably won't come back. I can sleep in the daylight. With the sounds of people outside.

I keep myself going with the distractions of life. I mean, you know, when you're walking down the street you don't think of continuous abuse. Or the discontinuity between what all the people around you think and what's true.

And sometimes a lorry will pass, and the sound exactly matches the sound of their approach, just for a moment, a discrete package of sound that makes me yell and start to move. My fight or flight instinct has been activated. I think sometimes they like to do that. To have me leap up when the combat music begins. But the sound of their approach is a steady sound, made of several sound packages back to back, or looped. It is a roaring. Not a roar.

Having yelled, I stop, and pant, and look for the mirror on the side of the lorry's cab to see that it's the driver inside, looking straight ahead, and not them playing with me.

Running through the streets of this city. Running as fast as I can, but I'm moving too slowly, it feels like my legs are moving through mud or water.

The screen freezes. I replace the batteries in the controller. My fifth set in this session.

I run up to a guard by the gate, and engage him in pointless conversation to push at my Speechcraft. His face is impassive, unmoved, but underneath he likes me. Doesn't like me. Likes me. 'You look like you know how to handle a blade.'

Through the gate, with another moment of darkness and discontinuity, another crashing sound, and then running again, running over the hills, with the sunlight and the flowers.

I look up, and there's the moon, but it's all right. It's not the real moon. If I could fly, and I can't in this game, I would reach a limit. The words would appear on the screen as they do beside that particular river or in those mountains. 'Turn back, you can go no further.' There is a roof up there. A blessed roof.

There's something on the edge of the sound all around me. A roaring –

But no, coming over the next hill, it's just a waterfall. It is just a waterfall.

Another city, another building, another crash, another sudden rush of an individual towards me. I'm ready for those now, I'm in charge, storming from place to place, my boots barely touching the tops of the rocks. I've burst into his house. No attempt at stealth this time.

This is a man in a hood. I can't see his eyes. That worries me. I don't know what his eyes might be like under there. 'Hello, outlander,' he says.

His name is Senior Steward. It sounds like a title, but he definitely looks like the sort of individual who is an individual, who will say specific and not generic things.

Do I want to talk about:

'Strangers in the City.'

'Find a Bed.'

'Rape.'

I look hard at the screen. Does that say 'rope'? I lean close, so I can see individual pixels. The dots of red, green and blue form an A.

I lean back. What a terrible typo. Someone should know about that. That should be all over the internet. Why haven't I heard about that?

I hit the line of text.

'You look like someone,' says the hooded man on the screen, in that cultured, rich voice that belongs to so many of the men, 'who is interested in rape.'

I find that my mouth is open. I'm shaking my head.

I have options.

'Yes, tell me more.'

'No, that's completely wrong.'

'Never mind how I feel. What do you mean?'

I stand up, feel all those muscles move that I haven't moved in hours. I have pins and needles in my left foot all of a sudden now. It takes me a couple of moments to get going, hopping.

I walk around the room, not looking back at the screen, touching things. I have to do that sometimes. I touch things with my palm, because grabbing things, while grounding me, reminding me of where I am, reminds me also of the times when I have felt I've had to grab things, to hold on. To uselessly fail to hold on. Or to grab something reflexively in helpless pain.

Touching things with the tips of my fingers reminds me of them.

Why did I stop? Because of those words.

I need to keep going. I don't want to be out here, I want to be in there. So why is that in there?

It's 3.33 am. They probably won't be coming back for me now.

The man on the screen waits, his eyes not visible. He shifts a little. I half expect him to look up at me, rather than at where I was sitting.

I wait for him to do that.

He doesn't.

I look away on purpose. Then look back.

He is still looking forward.

It's like this got into that. That world is getting to be like this one. Am I going to be left without anywhere to hide?

I can do the other thing that I do when I need to ground myself.

I reach under the bed, and pull out the bag. The bag used to contain a vibrator, handcuffs, chains that went from wrist to bedpost. But I couldn't bear them any more. I couldn't bear her smell on the vibrator, or the vibrator itself. How it felt to my fingers now. Soft and hard. Now the bag only contains books. Porn. Erotic novels. I haven't read any of them from start to finish, I don't think anyone does. But the narratives are familiar through repetition, and repetition is good, narratives, apart from the obvious narrative that is continually happening to me, are good. Having an erection seems to be the most grounding thing of all. It seems to sort of hold them off. All these books are about domination, one way or another. It's hard to find any that aren't.

There's a kind of standard narrative in these books. It's easy to pick out, because the filler's not read by anybody, it's virtual, it needn't be there. So you tend to hit the main points and see the similarities. A girl has a dull ordinary life. She yearns for something, she doesn't know what. She encounters someone from outside that life, who shows her a chink in the mirror. She's abducted into that other life, usually becoming a full time slave to a powerful organisation. Every now and then, because I think it's probably the law, she's asked if she wants to do this. And, though part of her doesn't, part of her, and I think it's probably the same part that translates pain into pleasure for a series of mysterious orgasms under the whip, makes her say yes. Often, by the end of the book, she's eager to do this to others. It's a romantic fantasy of Stockholm Syndrome.

It's strange that that law about what you can say in books exists, because one of the attractions of these for me, instead of visual pornography that is, is that nobody is hurt in the making of them. The girls are virtual. They exist in my head when I open the book, and have no life when I close it. If she said 'no' and meant it, nobody actual would be being hurt. Nobody would be being raped.

I stop. The thought has stopped me. Suddenly I can't sit here doing this in response to that. I have had the book open in my hand with my other hand on my cock for... for some unit of time now that I'm not entirely sure of, but it feels too long. And I'm flaccid. And can't be any other way now.

I put the book back in the bag, zip it up, and push it back under the bed.

I go back to the screen. He's still standing there, waiting for me.

I should say no, that's completely wrong.

But that's not true. I do have an interest in rape.

I have to be true to myself. If the world itself isn't true, then I, inside the world, have to be a true thing. I have to examine myself, and to tell myself the truth about myself.

I sit back down. I flex my fingers, and then look away from them. I hit the yes option.

'Then you should follow me,' he says. 'If you wish to.'

He goes to the door, and vanishes with the sound of the door slamming.

I follow. I'm shaking.

The darkness and loading screen seems to take forever

this time, the graphic moving along the bar inch by inch.

Until, with a crash of the door, I'm outside, and he's striding off across the night time grass lands. I wonder where he's going to take me. I have to follow.

I catch up to where the cursor indicates that I can Talk to Senior Steward, and try to.

'No time now,' he says. 'They will be on their way.'

There are all sorts of things I want to say. I sometimes come across a dead person and want to find someone and explain to them that I didn't do it. Now I want to ask if we're fleeing something or heading for something. In which of those two ways is it necessary for me to be interested in rape?

Ahead I see a glow through the trees. And the roaring sound. Growing louder. We are heading for a waterfall.

I slow down. He stops. He does not turn around. I'm looking at the back of his head.

I want to reach out and pull down his hood, but that's not one of my options. I could try to attack him, but I don't know how strong he is. I try not to attack anyone stronger than I am or weaker than I am.

The glow is leaking through those trees.

The glow gets stronger, and suddenly I want to get up from where I'm sitting again. But where is safe? No, it must be okay. This world is limited, just a construct: a series of finite options. There are designers involved here, I could look up their names in the instruction booklet. I must have stumbled on some sort of forbidden level, and I'm probably going to see, well, violent porn of some kind.

I'll report that. Kids play this. If I see that I'll make whoever's made it pay.

The glow resolves itself into a pulsing, silver then red lozenge, lying on the very normal rather English grass and out of place amongst the lovely trees. There are Primroses at its base that I could pick for their nectar.

I'm only slightly afraid of it. Because this is not part of

my experience, I've never seen one of these from outside. They seem nothing to do with what happens to me. Unless where I'm taken to is inside one. They are an item from the mythology of which I have no experience. A block of scenery that indicates a scenario but doesn't contribute to the narrative.

My guide stops beside the lozenge.

He turns suddenly to me and I flinch again. 'He is waiting for you inside.'

I move forward to what announces itself as 'Human Interior'. I click to enter Human Interior. The darkness and not a clunk now but... was that a low level sort of grunt, like the sound of a bruise?

The interior is just darkness. I click to the map option, and find... empty space. No boundaries. The little box that indicates the entrance to something. But it's not labeled. I aim for that. I walk a while.

Something is ahead of me.

Then... has the screen switched off? I'm suddenly in darkness. I'm looking at the screen. I'm looking at a mirror. I'm looking at me.

'Hello,' he says. He has my voice.

I hit the button to talk, and find the options:

'Fine structure.'

'Rape.'

'The nature of the universe.'

I hit 'fine structure'.

'Following inflation,' he says, in my voice, like he's performing this line by line but is too professional not to feign interest. 'The stronger, inward gravitational force was defeated by the weaker, outward gravitational force that you now live with.' He makes it sound like a legendary battle of myth. 'In the first moment, the designers worked on the ocean of the Higgs Field, and divided the large scale from the small scale.'

A new sentence is highlighted now. 'The big bang.'

'It happened yesterday. At every point in your universe. It will keep happening. Memory and history can be switched on and off.'

I'm back to the original set of options. I hit 'the nature of the universe.'

'Time was created in this process. For those inside your universe, therefore, the only option is death.'

I'm crying and I don't know why. I hit 'rape'.

I sometimes find myself looking hard at the image of myself in the mirror. I'm waiting for it to change. I'm waiting for the things which wait behind every wall to be seen through them. Sometimes on nights when I can feel the pressure, when I'm waiting to hear the sound begin, first in the background and then ever closer, the continuing waterfall that's happening to me, I just look and look at the most everyday things: a chair; the corner of a newspaper; the pattern in the wood, waiting, certain, expecting now, for the details to resolve themselves into their eyes, their faces, their laughter.

Ha ha ha, they go, like they're reading their lines, with no emotion that reaches deeper than what they're reading next, ha ha ha.

I sit there, the sinews in my neck straight, ready for them, waiting for them to casually walk around the corner of the doorframe in my lounge, thin as a shadow. But they don't. They've trained me to wait for the sound. I am their story of O.

'If rape is a lack of options,' I say, 'the nature of the universe is rape.'

Perhaps it's about being born. I find myself wiggling my stunted arms and legs, which makes them laugh. Ha ha ha. I go through somewhere dark and somewhere light. There are birthing moments, me going into and out of things, and things going into and out of me. I am made to gasp like the victim of violent porn, I am covered in fluids.

Nobody asks what car crashes are 'about'. Those are allowed to happen to us. We're allowed to relate how they happened in history, in memory, what they mean to us. I wish one of those would happen to me.

I look at myself. 'Yes?' I say.

I've exhausted all the still lit options on the screen. I go into Speechcraft mode, and see how much I like me. I try and raise it using the Speechcraft skill. 'That's just ridiculous,' I say. 'I don't believe you.' 'Are you threatening me?' 'That way of thinking only leads to suicide.'

I realise I could do this. I draw my sword.

He draws his.

I'm better than him, I knock him this way and that in the dark space. I block his attacks. He can't block mine. Finally, he falls.

'You are unconscious,' the screen says.

I'm looking at my reflection in the screen.

I don't know how long it's been off. None of the lights are on. The clock radio's off. I don't know what time it is. There must have been a power cut.

I can't hear anything from the street outside. I will look out of the window. I make myself look towards the window. There's no face there. There's just the usual frame, windows opposite. The usual picture.

I make myself get up. I scuttle. I go and look closer. I put my face to the glass, and I see myself looking back there too. I look closer at the view of the house opposite, and I can see the fine detail, the red and green dots, of my own face.

The sound has started. The waterfall.

My fingers slip against the glass.

It gets as loud as it gets. I make myself turn and look towards the doorway.

I look and I look.

And finally there he is. Walking around the doorframe.

And then suddenly in front of me. Erect.

'Ha ha ha,' he says.

A cut scene follows. I am flown into a dark space, then a light, and spread-eagled. Everything in the room swings around me.

He is framed looking down at me from behind. 'We are here to penetrate you unto death.'

I have three options to reply.

'Yes.'

'Yes.'

Or 'yes.'

The Deadly Space Between

CHAZ BRENCHLEY

'Hey, he's asking for you again.'

I smiled, ducking my head down in hopes they wouldn't see. Probably too late. Probably pointless anyway; bodies talk as loud as faces. Everyone has expressive shoulders and a giveaway spine.

I didn't need to pretend, then. For sure, I didn't need to say, 'Who's asking?' I just put down the frame I'd been building, cleared my mess away with that swift neatness that comes from sharing, picked up my toolbox and walked out. It's strange how really, really hard it is to walk, to remember how you do that normal thing, when half of you wants to saunter for the sake of whoever's watching, the other half wants to scurry for the sake of what's to come.

What that might be today, I didn't try to guess. I only skipped towards it like a child anticipating treats. Even knowing that treats always, always disappoint in the end, I was still skipping.

Take a flour mill and gut it, rip out the silos, take it all the way back to a shell; then let the old bricks hold something they can never contain. A hollow space, an art space, bright and clean and pure; let all the work be new, sharp, unresolved, light at the speed of thought.

The Mill wasn't a gallery so much as a factory, a space where art needed making. The crew was there to help. I'd swept a lot of floors, painted a lot of walls; or swept the same floors, rather, painted the same walls, over and over again. And made a lot of boxes, humped a lot of stuff around, framed and hung and rehung an inch one way, an inch the other; spent days up ladders, running cables and pointing lights. I was a stagehand, perhaps, in a play without actors. At the Mill, it was all about setting scenes.

Until Case came, and made me feel like I'd been pulled out onto the stage, with all the lights turned on me.

Case had the secret room, an unexpected space up between one level and the next, that seemed to have taken even the architects by surprise. It wasn't meant for exhibitions, but Case – well, he came and looked and said 'I'll do it here,' so that was that. Anything Case wanted, was the rule.

Which was of course why Case could ask for me and get me, every time. Hell, I was just following rules.

I followed the rules all the way up to the secret room. We still called it that, though it wasn't much of a secret any more. You just had to know the way, through the library and up a narrow staircase. Arranging public access, managing the traffic was going to be tricky.

Not my problem, though. Case was my problem, seemingly, if he was anybody's. If he was a problem. Others said so. I said as little as possible, and never mind what the whole Mill was saying behind my oh-what-a-giveaway back.

The door was closed, as always. I knocked, as always, and waited till he called me in.

It was a square box of a space, windowless and spare, hanging indeterminately between two floors. Case inhabited that space like a bird confined, angular and pacing. He didn't make things easy for himself, nor for the rest of us. Why should he? Case wasn't only famous among artists, or among those people who cared about art. He'd transcended his own world.

What he did was news, what he made mattered. People who had never been inside a gallery, never stopped to look at a sculpture in the street, they still had opinions about Case.

I had opinions about Case, but they didn't matter. Opinion was random, unless it was his own. It wasn't that he was self-centred, or even self-obsessed; he was self-focused, all his attention turned inward because that was where art came from, his art, which was all the art that mattered.

Or maybe I'd missed the point, maybe he really was the monster that others called him. That didn't matter either. The work made the grief worthwhile, for director and crew. For the tabloids, for their readership, for all the world outside the Mill, it seemed as though the grief – all the tantrums, the acid tongue, the unreasonable demands and brutal public judgements – made the work worthwhile; worth making a fuss over, at any rate.

For me, the man himself was justification enough for both. I didn't care how great the art or how egotistical the artist, so long as he would let me be there.

Sometimes not. Some days he closed himself into the room and let no one in, asked for nothing, never asked for me. Today, he yelled me in as soon as I knocked and waved an impatient hand at my toolbox, 'Drop that in a corner, you won't need it. We're going out.'

'I can take it back to the workshop...'

'Leave it, I said. It'll be safe, I'm locking up.'

Of course he was locking up. He'd fitted hasps and staples to the door and used his own padlocks, not trusting any lock for which someone else might have a key. We were used to eccentricities, but we'd never had to deal with this degree of paranoia. Even the director didn't know what Case was creating. I was the only one allowed in, and he didn't talk art to me. He talked practicalities – projectors and screens and speakers, black hangings, acoustic baffles, an airlock-style double door – and he asked about life, life in the city, my life.

What sketches and plans I had seen, I couldn't understand. He used a kind of visual shorthand, where a few scribbled lines on a vast sheet of paper made a storyboard. The crew nagged at me, even the director asked me about it more than once; I could say it was video, audio, no more than that, and they knew that much already. He had a secret space in his head, I thought, that he kept more thoroughly locked up than he did ours.

His shoes squeaked on polished wood as we walked out of the studio; my boots clattered on galvanised steel as we went downstairs. He said, 'I'm fascinated by the sounds of this building, the way it interacts with us when we move, whenever we move; it has so many voices.'

I was learning to listen to the spaces around his words, the meanings he didn't trouble to articulate. 'We can put down rubber,' I said, 'when you're ready to open. Doesn't matter what people wear, their shoes won't make a noise.'

He nodded, almost satisfied. 'Black rubber.'

'Of course.'

He had read about the city, watched videos, listened to me talking. No doubt he'd listened to others too. He was crisply blond going to grey, I was sandy and stubble-cut, and I'd found dark hairs on the pillows in his courtesy flat. I changed the sheets and asked no questions. Now he was ready to look at the city itself, to listen to the streets. He wouldn't go unmediated, though, he still wanted me as a guide. I didn't feel flattered, Case didn't deal in flattery; mostly I felt challenged, stretched, tugged into a world more adult and more demanding than I could ever be ready for.

And thrilled to be there, of course, and excited beyond measure, lurching from mute to madcap and cursing myself for both: for giving myself away so thoroughly under those cruel, casual, experienced eyes, for looking and acting and sounding so unbearably, so unforgivably young.

Case had never been young. I was sure of that. Surely no child could ever have lived behind those eyes. He must have been made man-size, already understanding how to look at the world, already knowing how to shape people to his art or to his pleasure.

He shaped me, whichever way he wanted to. I'd have remade my body if I could, stretching my legs to match his, so that I could meet him eye to eye. Except that he might not have liked that. He seemed to appreciate me as I was, scurrying where he stalked and always looking up.

I took him places where he had to look up himself, where the steep river-valley and centuries of engineering had laid the city down in strata, so that we walked in the shadows of bridges and climbed steps to church. I took him to the castle, of course, and the railway station too; to Chinatown and the mediaeval walls, an odd surviving touch of the Roman wall and so back down past the cathedral to the river.

Climbing the complex curves of the new bridge, he paused to lean on the rail and look upriver, all the bridges in line abreast. I copied him, of course I did; I had no personality to call my own, so long as I stood in his shadow.

'Glory be to God for dappled things.'

I was looking at sunlight on broken water as the tide backed up, and he gave me the words for it. I glanced round, grateful and amazed – and found that he was only looking at the freckles on my arms.

'Come,' he said, 'we'll go back to the apartment.'

'I don't know, Case. I do actually have a job, the crew expects me to show up now and then...' And would know just what to think when I didn't. And would say so, loudly, often.

'I am your job, for now,' he said. And he was right, of course; and we did what he wanted, of course, then as ever.

And came back to the Mill afterwards, of course, because it

was still and all about the art; and he let us both into the secret room, and we stood there gaping. At least, I was gaping. Case was shaken, shaking, furious.

'Who has been in here?'

It was a rhetorical question, necessarily. I couldn't give him an answer. Instead, I did the only thing I could think of; I fetched the director, at a run.

'Case, you say someone's been here, but I don't see...'

'This is not my work!' with a wave of his long hand at the wall, where a dozen sheets of roughs were pasted to the paintwork.

'Is it not? It has your copyright stamp, on every sheet...'

'Yes, yes. I mean I did not put these sheets into this order, nor did I glue them to the wall there.'

I could have confirmed that, if either of them had asked me. When we'd left, those roughs were with the others, all stashed in his portfolio.

'Well, but you know none of us can open this door once you've locked it.'

'Then there must be another way in.'

'How?' she asked, and he had no answer for her. Me neither. No windows in the space, no trapdoors in the floor, no service hatches in the concrete walls or ceiling. We had a locked-room mystery of the worst kind, with no solution. No space for exotic theories or extravagant guesswork, nothing to work with. Just the blank canvas, the thing itself. The director said nothing, too canny to risk losing him, but I knew what she was thinking: that he'd given keys to someone else. Maybe for precisely this effect, to make this fuss? It made no sense, but it was something to believe. What Case believed, I couldn't start to guess.

He couldn't be mollified, she couldn't be persuaded; I couldn't have found a more awkward place to stand, between the two of them. Worse than that, though, I gazed at what had happened, someone else's hand in Case's precious work, and I thought about the impossibility of that, and I could feel something terrible building at our backs. Trouble to come: I don't know why I should have felt it was behind us, like a great storm pushing, pushing.

Trouble was, Case didn't rip the sketches and storyboards down from the wall and start again, clean sheets with no one's fingerprints all over them. Once he'd stopped being angry, he just stood and looked at what the intruder had done. For a long time he stood there, and then he grabbed a handful of coloured markers and starting scribbling, adding hasty designs, drawing arrows that looped across the wall to link one frame with another.

I didn't say anything, I only watched from my corner, but I'd gone all premonitory again, I thought this was such a really, really bad idea.

I didn't speak, I didn't move, it took him a long time to notice me at all. When he did, he just said, 'Are you still here?'

So then I wasn't: not then, and not later. Next time I passed the director on the stairs, she stopped me. 'I don't suppose he gave you a second set of keys, did he?'

'I was with him, all the time we were out.'

'Yes, but you might have passed them on to someone else.'

I supposed I might. I smiled politely, and said, 'No, he never gave me a set of keys.' Not to the secret room, not to the flat. 'Me of all people, he never would. He wouldn't let anyone that close.'

'Ah, you might be right. I'm sure you are. I'm sorry.'

What she was sorry for, she didn't say. I didn't ask.

Even the crew can be sensitive, when a thing just isn't funny any more. After a few days they stopped teasing, they stopped asking how Case was or what he was up to. They knew as much as I did, exactly as much: he was busy, feverish, out in the city with digital video equipment or else holed up in his increasingly secret room with a portable editing suite and the occasional sandwich, the odd bottle of beer sent up from the café.

Not me, but some people listened at the door if they just happened to be passing. They heard street noise, they reported, voices and traffic and such.

If you turned off the lights in the stairwell, they said, accidentally while he was still working, you could sometimes see a video flicker round the frame of the door.

The next time I went up there, it wasn't Case who sent for me, it was the director. Me and my toolbox, please.

The door was open, so I didn't knock; they were having a fight, or at least Case was, so I almost didn't go in. In the end, I sidled into my corner again.

Nostalgia means a return to pain. Like picking off a scab too soon, I guess. I focused on what they were saying. What she was saying, rather; he was shouting.

'It's health and safety, Case, it's the law...'

'Art is not required to be healthy, and it should never be safe!'

'That's fine to tell the critics, but it's not much good when the inspectors come to renew our certificates. I'm sorry, Case, but the sign goes up over the door here before we even talk about what else needs doing.'

What it was, it was the emergency exit sign. He wanted darkness, pure dark except for the work itself; he couldn't have it. Too bad. I fetched steps, and got on with my job while he fumed below. When I was finished, I left. He didn't say a word.

'So what are you saying, then, you think it was a ghost?'

'No, of course not. But if no one else had keys, and there's no other way in – well, what else have you got?'

'Me? Nothing. Okay, let's run with this. The secret room is haunted. The ghost must've been here before we were, while the Mill was still milling; no one's died since, that I know of. So, what, did someone drown in a flour barrel?'

'Choke, surely – too dry to drown. And I don't know, but there must've been accidents. Try the Journal.'

'Try the web first. But whoever died and however they did it, they didn't do it in the secret room. It wasn't there, it's an invention of our architects. So why would your ghost be haunting that? And how come it knows about art, what Case needs to do, where his piece is going?'

'It's not my ghost, don't call it mine. All I'm saying is, eliminate the impossible, and see what you're left with.'

'Ghosts are eliminated before the whistle. They are impossible. Someone's got a set of keys and they're lying about it. Embarrassed at being quicker than the big man, to see what the work needed. Drop him a big hint and then keep shtum; do it secretly and don't claim credit, it's all for the art.'

'Really? Who'd do that, then?'

'Someone who cared. It's just a pity Case can't do gratitude. The man's a shit, I got that off the web. Not that I needed to. Just look around, see who he doesn't notice any more.'

'Oh, hey, he doesn't notice any of us.'

'That's my point.'

Another day, another doubt. Case had changed the locks, but between night and morning somehow half his recordings apparently got themselves wiped. Software glitch, power spike, some random magnetic event? Even the director didn't quite dare to suggest artist error. Case said it was deliberate; he could tell by the distribution, what had been deleted and what remained.

What interested the crew was what he didn't say. Not sabotage, not vandalism, no mention of damage, disaster, abandonment, starting again. Once past the shock, the outrage of it all, he seemed content with the choices made for him.

Back came the ghost, into workshop conversation all around me:

'It's the Phantom of the Flour-Mill, it's got to be. Leaving his powdery footprints at the scene of crime, I expect. It's a spooky conspiracy; Dusty does the work, and Case gets the credit.'

'Ah, but I don't think it's our ghost at all, I think it's his. I think he brought it with him.'

I thought it best just to keep quiet, keep my head down, do my job. I took to wearing a Walkman while I worked, not to hear all their happy speculation.

Then Case announced that he was ready. I had to go back in, but at least this time I could go with the crew, part of the team.

We built a lobby and a second door, to give him his airlock effect. We padded walls and ceiling with egg-box foam and painted everything black, to swallow light and sound. We fed in all the cables that he needed, for his projectors and speakers and the black boxes that would run the show; we fitted infra-red eyes on the doors, though he didn't tell us why. He didn't tell us anything. We still didn't know what the piece was about. Why should we? We were only crew.

Except that when I was up on the steps fixing a speaker bracket, I felt fingers circle my ankle in a casual, teasing grip. I knew they were his. I always knew exactly where he was in the room. Right now he was below me, and there might be a monstrous arrogance in that touch but it still burned on my bare skin, and there might be a heedless mockery in his voice but it still carried all the shiver, all the tingle that ever it had.

'Come to the apartment tonight. We'll have a celebration. In the morning, you can be first to see what I have made.'

And I said, 'Yes, Case. Thank you. I'd like that,' and what I meant was *it'll be an honour*, and he heard that and agreed with it.

Then he moved away. I still wasn't looking down, and I couldn't hear his footsteps on the thick rubber matting, but I knew just when he left me, and how far he went. When I felt another grip on my ankle, I had time enough to be startled first and then bewildered, time to think *no, not him*, time almost to wonder why I was so shivery when it wasn't him, before that grip tightened and tugged and pulled me clean off the steps.

No time to look, to see who had me; I was falling, hard and fast, and swearing all the way.

Rubber matting was better than cedarwood floor to fall on, but I still didn't bounce. Crunched, rather.

Then everyone else was swearing, clamouring around and above me, while I was suddenly the quiet one and lying remarkably still.

It was Case who hushed them, who crouched down beside me, who said, 'Can you move?'

I flapped a vague hand at him, more to reassure myself. My head buzzed strangely, vivid shadows were closing in; I could feel my mouth working, but I couldn't find the air. It seemed an age before the clench below my ribs unfolded slowly like a fist, and my lungs could catch.

'Easy,' Case said. 'You knocked all the wind out of yourself. What hurts?'

'Everything.' Or nothing, yet, but everything was making promises for later.

As he chuckled and I wasn't conspicuously oozing gore, the crew was moving on from worry to curiosity, asking what happened, why I'd fallen. I glowered up at them muzzily and said, 'Somebody pulled me, that's why. One of you,' as I knew it wasn't Case.

'That's not true. We saw, and there wasn't anyone near when you went. You just toppled sideways, all of a sudden.'

'Somebody pulled me, I felt it. I felt their hand, around my ankle,' and I felt the abrupt stillness of Case's hands on my ribs.

'You couldn't have,' they insisted. 'Truly. You just went, is all.'

Once I was upright, Case prescribed painkillers, anti-inflammatories and an afternoon in bed. His bed: he gave me the keys.

'I can't come,' he said, 'we have to get finished here today. Someone will go in the taxi with you. If you feel sick, if you feel dizzy, call. Otherwise rest, and I will see you when we're done.'

I did go to bed, I did sleep for an hour or two, and woke feeling worse than before, stiff and sore and uncertain. I had a bath, long and deep and luxurious; then I pulled on his own bathrobe, also long and deep and luxurious, and migrated all through the flat from TV to CD rack to bookshelves before at last I landed up at the computer, where probably I'd been headed all the time.

If you google Case, you get literally thousands of results. I'd done it dozens of times already, at the Mill and at home, even occasionally right here while he slept. If he ever found my trail, I figured he'd be flattered or amused or just take it as a given, as his right, to be stalked across the internet; of course I'd be obsessed with him, how not?

Every time but this, though, I'd stayed within the semi-official record, the most popular or most respected sites. This time, I went further and dug deeper. *The man's a shit, I got that off the web* – I might have a gift for silence, but it's strictly one-way, I still know how to listen.

And I know how to look, on the web as well as in a gallery. What I found was a series of weblogs, the young and damaged bringing all their hurt and bewilderment to their natural court, that enfolding comfort that is cyberspace.

Slow conversations in the dark, and there was nothing new in them, nothing surprising. Great artists, great egotists have always treated their servants and disciples this badly. Fresh sex in every town and all the convenience of a local lover, companionship and admiration and no ties, just walk away when it's over – why wouldn't they?

Shame on us for not seeing how well we fitted the pattern, how easy we made it for him. Except that there was one not fitting now, one who'd dropped out: I found half a dozen broken links, to a journal that had been deleted.

Reading between the lines of others' entries was not difficult, and I confirmed the facts from a newspaper's online archive. One of his conquests, Jan Sommers, hadn't survived the encounter. Twenty-four years old, bright and beautiful, betrayed like all of us, Jan had said goodbye in a weblog entry, swallowed a handful of mixed prescriptions and jumped from a high bridge to make assurance doubly sure, an endless fall into the dark.

I tried to blame it on my state of mind, still shaky from my own fall, maybe a little concussed; but a long slow soak in a hot bath hadn't been able to wash away the feel of cold fingers around my ankle. And Case's workplace had been twice locked, and twice invaded; and I didn't know what else had happened, here or elsewhere, that we hadn't been told; and I wasn't the first whose thoughts had fallen this way. *I don't think it's our ghost at all, I think it's his. I think he brought it with him.*

I thought so too. I didn't know that it was Jan, but I thought it might be. I was sure that Case would know, except that I couldn't ask him.

That evening, a call on my mobile:

'Hullo, Case.'

'Where are you? I told you to wait for me, here at the apartment...'

'I'm fine,' though he hadn't asked. 'I just wanted my own bed, that's all. I came home.'

'Ah. Well then, sleep sweetly. Will you come to the Mill in the morning? I do want you to be first to see the work.'

I wasn't sure why he'd want that; I wasn't at all sure why I'd ever want to go near that room again. But I was still susceptible, still half slave to his charisma. Of course I said yes, I couldn't not.

'Good, then. I'll be waiting.'

He was; I saw him watching for me through the windows of the café. We didn't say much. He just took me up to the secret room, stood back and waved me in.

The first door, black and heavy, revealing nothing. I passed on into the little lobby-space we'd made, and let it swing shut behind me. Here there was leakage, there was the tinny drone of a soundtrack muffled but not altogether contained by the second door; there was the flickering, tentative backlight of a projection showing between that door and its frame.

As I pushed it open, the sound and the projection both cut off. I stepped forward into silence, into darkness, into a space that spoke of secrets and sudden absence.

The door closed behind me. I waited, and nothing happened. Absolutely nothing, neither art nor accident.

I waited until it would have been simply foolish to wait

any longer. The door had its exit sign, glowing greenly where I'd hung it; despite Case's resentment, it felt like a part of the work.

I went back through, felt it close at my back and caught the first flickers of light around its edges, heard the soundtrack start again before I opened the second door and stepped out.

Perhaps it was my eyes, dazzled from the dark; for a moment, I thought Case looked massively, monstrously relieved just to see me.

Then, the artist in him: 'Well?' he said.

To be perverse, I said, 'I think it's broken. Nothing happened, it switched off the moment I went inside and didn't start up again till I came out.'

'It's meant to do that. That's what it's about, the space between eavesdropping and experience, the unknowability of other people's lives. We all live on the edge of the dark; here you can step over that edge, and still recover. It's about sleep, death, amnesia, all manner of loss...'

I thought it was about Jan Sommers, and so, I thought, did Jan. I thought Jan had helped to make it so.

'What's it called?'

'There is no title. How can you give a name to a place, a space that has none? I'm going in now. Wait for me in the café.'

'What,' I said slowly, 'you mean you haven't seen it yourself yet?'

'No. Last night, when everything was in place, I switched it on and left it; no one has been through the doors since. I said, you were to be the first.'

I was the sacrifice, he meant, to test how safe it was in there. I felt more like a Judas goat, who leads the sheep to slaughter. I thought I'd been let pass by.

I didn't go down to the café. I sat on the stairs and waited. In ones and twos, the crew came up to join me; after a while, so did the director.

We waited a long time, till it was clear that something had happened. *Art or accident*, I thought, grimly justified.

We called his name from the landing there, then from the lobby beyond the first door. There was no response, only the lights and noise of his artwork looping around. So we went inside, and couldn't find him in the dark. We'd taken all the lights away, at his insistence; someone ran for a torch, but we still couldn't find him.

At first they said it was a publicity stunt, the press and the police both. Then they thought it was a crime. Now they call it a mystery, and we get private detectives, relatives, psychics all coming to the Mill to locate him.

They're wasting their time. I know where he is. He's in the space he made between what we see and what we know, between art and actuality; the space where Jan was waiting, to pull him in.

I don't know, but I think it must be like falling: like falling and falling, with forever still to fall.

What I do know, what I'm sure of, is that when we take his artwork down, he's never ever going to find his way back out again.

By the River

MARIA ROBERTS

Summer came last March, now the temperature is unbearable. At first people went out in their thousands to buy paddling pools, hosepipes and water pistols. Woolworth's bragged that sales figures outstripped any other year. *The Messenger* printed photographs of a man cooking up a full English breakfast on the bonnet of his car. Joe next door claimed that if you left a pan of water outdoors long enough it would come to the boil. On the streets, kids in swimming costumes flung water at one another. Mum's best friend bought an enormous inflatable waterslide which we ran up and slid down time after time.

By June the flowers in the garden wilted, the grass parched. Everywhere was scorched and dry. Other gardeners soaked their lawns at night whilst we looked on in horror. When reports of babies and the elderly dying made headline news, Mum rationed our water and stockpiled on food. She put a brick in the cistern and insisted we flushed the toilet only once a day. She drank one cup of tea in the morning and put two litres of water in the fridge. We brushed our teeth at the same time and stopped washing our hair. We showered once a week – if Mum were thinner she would have insisted we did this together too – I felt and smelt rank so I covered myself in scented creams and perfume.

When temperatures hit 34°C we counted the days without rain. On day 26 the government officially announced the start of the drought. In the following weeks swimming pools were emptied and rallies were organised outside golf courses. Mum and I signed up on a roster to keep an eye on the golf course near us. It was a 24 hour vigil. I wanted to catch someone switching on the sprinklers, but no one did. Hefty fines were imposed elsewhere. The courts made an example of a man in Hereford who jet-sprayed his drive. He got a £5000 fine. It was disastrous for farmers. It was disastrous for us all. The price of meat and vegetables rocketed. For the first time since I'd left school, we ate meatballs.

Mum started to talk about the drought of '76. 'This isn't unexpected,' she said. 'They knew two years ago we were heading for a drought.' She became agitated, 'They should have imposed restrictions months ago. Dry winters. Hot summers. They've known all along.'

She bought deep steel bins and began to fill them with water. She sealed the tops tight and stored them in the bathroom across the landing and in our bedrooms. Then she stocked up on sterilising tablets, cereals, dry breads and tinned food. When the floor space was filled she hid our supplies at the bottom of the wardrobes and in drawers. We stopped using our car. Mum siphoned the water from the radiator into a tub. I laughed at her neurosis.

Late July the water supply to homes was cut and the city council finally gave up hailing Manchester as 'The New Madrid'. One evening we watched North West Water install a standpipe on our street; soon a stream of people trailed from the corner shop, past the chippy and over to St Francis' Church, hands clutching containers to fill up at the tap. Mum joined the queue and sent me to Mo's newsagents to a get a paper: on the cover of *The Star* was a picture of a beer-bellied bloke in Sussex dousing water over a blonde page 3 girl. *The Manchester Evening News* ran a picture of a pilot, grinning maniacally, standing next to an unwashed plane; the wheels stuck fast in the sticky tar.

BY THE RIVER

Mum took a piece she'd cut and kept from *The Times* and sellotaped it to the living room window. 'Listen to this Jenny,' she said. 'From the horse's mouth: David King, director of water management for the Environment Agency.' She spoke loudly as we sat on the doorstep, soaking up the sun: 'Only careful conservation of water will save the region from the first standpipes in thirty years, yet people – especially in London – continue to run their taps as if there were an endless supply.' She shouted more loudly as people passed us to make their way to the standpipe. 'The message isn't getting through. People have the perception that there is a lot of water, yet we have less water per person than parts of the Sudan or the southern Mediterranean.' She turned to me: 'Do you know when he said that Jenny?' I said I didn't. 'May 2006,' she said it again more emphatically: '*2006,*' then stomped inside. I thought Mum was obsessed. When it came to the environment she was OCD.

Then the worst motoring accident of our times became the first of many. A car's tyres exploded on the M60. The crash caused a pileup. Traffic backed up onto the M61 and the M62, made worse by rubbernecking and knock-on accidents. Vehicles spun into barriers. Bodies spewed across embankments and carriageways. Similar accidents occurred on the M1, the M6 and the M25. Thousands of motorists were left stranded without water. Many who survived the accidents then died of dehydration. No-one could get water to the motorists. Hospital staff walked out. The BBC showed the injured pleading for help. Aerial pictures showed arteries in and out of the cities clogged with crushed cars and torn bodies thrust all over the place.

Fires raged on the motorways for days. The Home Office sent out the Green Goddesses to support the fire service. Helicopters droned through the sky. At first they put out the flames but when a surging hot wind turned into a dust devil, it picked up a spark spreading the fire elsewhere. On 6th

August, my birthday, Sherwood Forest, the New Forest and Chalkney Wood were still in flames.

Sanitation was our biggest worry: E coli, cholera. It wouldn't be long before we were faced with an epidemic. What were we supposed to do with our waste? The toilets had long since packed in. Mum made a toilet in the garden and we used a tissue to wipe alcohol over our hands. We caught people shitting and pissing anywhere. One day we found a human turd not far from the standpipe. Mum had gone on a course at the Centre for Alternative Technology and vaguely knew how to build a compost toilet. She called a meeting at the church hall. 'If we work in teams,' she said to me, 'we can get a block built in no time.' We waited for an hour and no one came. Mum went round knocking on doors. A man with a yapping dog told her to fuck off.

There was talk of living like the Americans do in summer. Those that had cellars moved the family downstairs and made basement apartments. Teams dug out shelters in the parks. One day when the heat ripped through the streets like fire, a family over on Alice Street were baked alive. The little boy had left his glasses on the windowsill; his Dad had left a newspaper on the floor. In the kitchen were stores of paint and aerosols. Onlookers said there'd been an enormous bang, followed by what looked like fireworks.

On Radio 4's *Frontiers* programme, a scientist claimed that the Earth's mantle was moving towards the surface, he said the heat was coming from below as well as above, and that we had '...peeled the Earth's crust away like an apple skin'. He claimed relentless excavations and rebuilding had caused ruptures and punctured hotspots in cities across the UK. In Manchester there were upwellings of hot mud like those in Indonesia. He told us to expect similar occurrences in Gateshead and Canary Wharf. A religious zealot said we were slipping into hell, adding it wouldn't be long before many Britons would disappear like the lost people of Sumatra.

On 5th September temperatures of 61°C were recorded in London and Bournemouth. The ground temperature in Manchester was an aching 58.

When the water ran out, hysteria travelled. The standpipe on our road shuddered one last time. Now all that comes from the taps is dirt. Those inland planned an exodus to the countryside where there were reservoirs and tarns. On the coast the panic of rising sea levels sent people heading for higher ground. Those in the hills defended their zones like forts. The nation was bracing itself for a catastrophe. The message from above was 'stay where you are'. But it was absolute chaos: tanks blocked the motorway slip roads; closer to home there were reports of vigilante snipers in the Peak District and the Lake District. In cities across the UK there were riots. At first looters raided shops. Then they raided homes. Army troops were sent to patrol the streets. A ring of steel locked us in.

From his Highland retreat Gordon Brown said it was 'a necessary act of containment' until a 'strategy' had been decided. There were marches across Britain. Activists sweltered to death. The public called for a referendum and propaganda followed media spin. Ministers claimed aid would cost billions. The war had bled the coffers. Did the nation want tax rises or tax cuts? It mattered little to us, without water, what was the economy? Brown added that some losses were inevitable. On a positive note, he promised that resources would be spent elsewhere: investment in deserted rural areas, old mining towns could be brought back to life: new schools in Swanwick, medical centres in Merthyr Tydfil. Talks were held with international companies and subsidies raised for the relocation of global businesses to poorer, developing areas. Commentators spoke of a cold war raging between the inlanders and the outsiders. Manchester was 'becoming tribal'. Then we lost the Scilly Isles, the Orkney Islands and the Isle of Wight. Sometime mid-September, when the sea swelled, London began to sink into the water.

From that point we knew we were on our own. The regional papers had long since packed up. We had relied on the media for updates; but when London slipped into the Thames, our contact with the world outside our estate went with it. Once Manchester had been international news, soon we were forgotten in the grand scale of it all. On the day we heard the last *World Service* bulletin, we hung around Mr Tatt's solar DAB radio like hornets. After the national anthem played, we were left with a lonely fizz. I thought about the tragedy in New Orleans: guilty for not caring more, remembering how I'd switched over from the scenes of people clinging to homemade rafts and swimming through their dining rooms, to watch reality TV.

We had plans of course. 'Our street is a street of survivors,' rallied Mum. 'What we need are workable solutions. Think. Think.' Joe next door suggested hauling carpets up onto the roof to soak up the sun. Mum was doubtful. 'I tried it with the rabbit hutch last summer,' he insisted, 'it works.' Once there, parched and disorientated, he stumbled and fell off. From the kitchen we heard the crack of his body as he flew from the chimney to the concrete path. Across the road Mr Tatt didn't make it down either. His body festered on the roof for weeks, attracting birds that considered him hearty carrion.

We had started cycling to my nana's on Sundays, taking her what little water and food we could hide on our bodies. We would take a path through Mersey Valley, following the river. Mum could do that journey blind. She'd ridden that way since she was a child. It was cooler along the bank than at home but the shadows made me twitch and shudder. I was frightened something would creep from the water, which trickled and ebbed with life. The trees creaked and sometimes I thought I heard what sounded like hissing or laughter. I rode nervously; people had been attacked for less.

Mum said it was the earth cooling down. She insisted we rode in silence.

The last night we saw Nana there was trouble in the playground across the road. From her window we saw a lynch mob strip five people from the waist up. Mum told me to go and hunt for Nana's slippers. Secretly, I watched from upstairs. I recognised a couple who lived over by the Co-op. The other winter they had helped Nana with her shopping when the car broke down and we couldn't get round. I thought they were being taught a lesson. I don't know, being beaten or something. It was dark and I couldn't quite see. The next morning we saw they had been strung from the railings by their wrists, a slit cut from nipple to nipple in a large boastful smile, their innards hanging out like a fat slathering tongue. A neighbour said they'd turned their outhouse into a sauna by tipping water over hot bricks. It had been Tessa's, the woman I recognised, fiftieth birthday.

The bodies hung there for days. The weeping flesh attracted flies. Mum and I didn't want to leave, but Nana insisted that we couldn't stay with her. 'I'd love you to stay, Jenny, I really would' she said, stroking my hair, 'but quite simply, there isn't enough food. I'll see you next Sunday.' She smiled at me, held my hand, pressed her fingers into my palm. Before we left Mum sealed the windows and vents for her. She was worried flies would get in, or worse. 'Make sure you lock the door Mum,' she called. 'Love you.' As we rode off, the bodies were being pulled down.

Back home Mum called another meeting at the church hall. This time twenty people turned up. 'Communication is important,' Mum bleated. 'Don't stay locked in your houses.' With those present she organised a biweekly expedition to the park where they would hunt for foliage and animals to eat. In the dark some pulled water from the river. The level was so low they drained sediment through a sock. Mum told them that the slurry was full of hard metals and poisons like arsenic, sulphur compounds and cyanide. She said she could teach them divination. Between them they could find cleaner sources of groundwater. She said there were a number of methods. If they could find a hazel tree then hazel branches were best, otherwise they could be made from metal rods. Mum used a rose quartz which hung around her neck. They accused her of witchcraft. Father Hoare said divination was Satan's work. 'Water companies have been losing billions of gallons a year,' Mum argued. 'They have pipes leaking all over the place; there will be water somewhere.'

The foraging group dismissed it as nonsense. They joked that soon she'd be showing them how to get water from a stone. Who did she think she was? Moses? Father Hoare said: 'If I die then so be it,' he stared at Mum, 'I'd rather not go to hell.'

On good nights the streets became lively again. Other nights silence smothered us all, like dread had started to pass from cell to cell. I thought we were on the brink of bedlam. Mum dismissed it as people coming to terms with those they had lost. One evening the forage was a huge success so we ate our finds together. Some kid played his guitar and Mum got them all dancing and singing. She had drilled it into me not to eat other people's food, but that night she took scraps from everyone, eager to make amends. I sat back and watched. All I could think was, cholera. Mum had warned me about cholera: I told her to stop – to come back home. 'Go to bed Mum,' I said. 'You're making a fool of yourself.' 'If you want to go home,' she hissed, 'you go home.'

It was only hours before she complained of aching legs. Then the vomiting began. Mum told me to get the spade and try and dig a hole at the far end of the garden. The ground was caked hard, it wouldn't give. 'A bucket,' she ordered, 'A container. Anything.' Fluid poured from her arse. I sifted through our supplies for sugar and salt. She ate it on tinned potatoes and breadsticks. I boiled and sterilized water from one of the steel bins. We had bottles of Coke stored for an emergency. I poured Mum pints of it, knocking out the gas with a spoon. Mum ordered me not to touch anything she had touched. Within two days half the estate was dead. Within a week Mum was on her feet again.

She cursed herself for being so stupid. We hoped Nana would be okay. Mum had taught her how to dowse for water how to reuse it, how to balance her diet, how to forage. Mum was a herbalist, an expert on edible plants and nutrition. She had drummed survival into us both. But that night, when we entered Nana's bedroom we found her body lifeless and emaciated, curled up in her bed. She had her favourite picture of me, Mum and Granddad tight in her fist. She was smiling, like she knew she was on her way out. There was food in the cupboards and she had a flask of water by the bed.

We set about digging a rough grave. Mum was a fascist about wasting water but she washed Nana's body with all the water she could find. She did Nana's hair nice and changed her into her favourite dress; the olive one Granddad loved her in. It was a struggle to get her body down the stairs. Mum was weak. She kept dropping Nana's legs. In the end I thumped her down one step at a time. In the garden Mum attempted the last rites then we shovelled the soil over Nana and left her there.

Mum gathered what tins were left in the cupboard and we set off back across Mersey Valley.

My bike struggled to navigate the paths. It seemed like the ground had moved. When something sped past me in the bushes I fell off. My legs scraped against the rough stones, my ankle wrangled in the frame. Mum was far behind, out of sight. A large figure loomed over me, masses of tangled hair falling over its face and shoulders. The stench was overwhelming. 'Get up,' it said. I scrambled trying to get my footing. I wanted to run. I tried to yell for help but nothing came out. 'Get up,' it said again. This time its thick hand tugged me from the ground. I kicked and hit out but it grabbed my wrists. It pulled me under the bridge then flung me down on a chair. It lit a lamp. In the candlelight I saw it was a man. 'Wait there,' he said. 'She'll ride this way soon.'

Mum rode past. I heard her shouting for me. When she saw us she gripped and shook me viciously. He pulled her off me, 'I'm Andrew,' he said shaking her hand. Mum thanked him for helping me and offered him water and food. Andrew refused, saying he'd already eaten. He pointed to the river and told us how the water level had dropped. I nudged and glared at Mum. She shouldn't encourage him: he could rape and dissect us at any moment.

Mum changed. Once she glided from place to place full of optimism. Now her blonde wavy hair was knotted and dirty, her face twisted and sore. Worn out she barely had the energy to repeat her daily mantra of 'Just wait for autumn to come.' We lost track of the days. We had no idea what month we were in, or whether we had entered a new year. We became night walkers. Those that wandered in the daytime looked like skinned rabbits. Red raw skin scabbed and scarred from the ever-blistering sun. From our house we could hear babies and children wail. The constant whine and relentless heat made my blood boil; when a cry was severed instantly Mum and I would look at one another and become still.

Out walking one night we found a man half-eaten by the pavement, like the ground had swallowed him and left the unwanted bit behind; one eye burst, his face wrung out with pain. We told Brian four doors down, he went to investigate but returned saying there was nothing there. His son Stephen headed off the next night and never returned.

The remaining members of the group began to comment how healthy we still looked. 'Your mum's recovery from cholera was remarkable,' said Sue. Whilst they marauded blistered and chaffed, half their body weight gone, bones sticking out and teeth decaying, we seemed almost plump. They noticed that whilst they scavenged, Mum and I hung back. We didn't fight for pickings, we waited our turn. I wanted to believe we were being paranoid but there was an unspoken understanding between Mum and I that we were in danger. Plans needed to be made. I could see it in the way Mum walked, the way she ate, how she smiled at me, how she watched me fall asleep from an uncomfortable chair, unable to rest.

Mum had wanted to share our food and water. 'But we're not the bloody Red Cross,' she'd decided. 'The Red Cross will do all that.' The Red Cross never came. We were fearful that if we distributed our stores, we'd be ransacked by gangs. We didn't have enough for everyone. There was only enough for us – and we were running short.

We salved our conscience with the knowledge that for years we'd been conserving water. Whilst they chucked it about, we gathered and reused it. We'd done our bit. If we seemed lucky, it was because we'd acted carefully whilst they threw it around like buffoons. Then there were other tactics. We collected our urine in jam jars and drank it. They peed into holes in the garden. Mum said, 'What a waste of minerals and B vitamins.' We collected and cooked our own faeces. Mum had seen it on a science programme. She said, 'Excrement is a complete meal. It contains all the excess nutrients your body didn't need first time round.' I retched more from the thought than the taste; which was indistinguishable. We cooked it on a fire then spread it on crackers.

We forced shit down ourselves once a week. Other times we ate worms, rats, insects and rough vegetation Mum knew our bodies could digest.

When Mum suggested drinking piss and eating shit to the foraging group they said unanimously that they would extinguish any offender. 'Cannibalism is a monster waiting for us all,' said Graham, 'and that is one step towards cannibalism.' We all denied cannibalism's attraction but you could see passersby eyeing up the recently dead that littered the streets. People hung about watching foxes, cats and dogs, as well as vermin, crows and magpies, tucking in and getting fat, whilst they starved.

We had a few tins but Mum rationed everything. We ate a chunk of fruit everyday, sometimes a potato and a spoon of beans. Compared to everyone else, we lived in luxury.

There was the feeling that our every move was being watched. Only last week the foraging group started going out without Mum and when we shouted hello from the door they ignored us. Yesterday I thought I saw a face at the bedroom window, an eye at the keyhole, a nose sniffing through the letterbox. Mum wouldn't leave me alone. Trouble was on its way. Our bodies felt it. Our skin pricked at the slightest sound. Mum took to holding me tightly whenever she could; kissing my head over and over. We caught a group hovering by the house, heard the sound of someone scrabbling over the fence and running away. Late last night we stuffed provisions in our pockets and headed to the bridge where Andrew lived. We replenished the water cans which he kept on a shaded shelf he'd constructed from rubbish.

Riding back from the bridge I sensed the river had finally dried up. The drone of flies was constant and deafening. It made my head throb. Back home Mum said to eat as much as I could. Pep up my energy. Prepare to flee. 'We must be strong,' she said. We limbered up in the living room. We listened to every sound, scrape, cough, and sneeze. I listened so closely I was certain I could hear our neighbours breathe. We kept the curtains closed. We spoke to no one.

Mum felt there was a change in temperature. For weeks she had been saying that things were going to change. That rain was coming. She gripped the rose quartz around her neck. 'It's vibrating,' she said. But I didn't believe her. She watched the tree outside our house. She was certain there was a hint of green; that buds were attempting to appear. This morning she stepped outside to investigate, wrapped up so tightly she could barely move in the heat. Her skin covered so as not to burn. She wore a floppy hat which fell over her eyes. I thought she looked prettier than she had in a long time.

Outside she shouted to the neighbours: 'Rain is on its way. Look!' She pointed to the clouds, 'Rain clouds.' There was a commotion. From the window I saw two men nod to one another. Mum looked relieved. 'I've appeased them at last,' she said, entering the house. But then I saw she had what looked like jam on her shirt.

We knew they'd be back. We heard the sound of a mob gathering at the end of the street. Their tools clanked on the pavement as they walked. Mum looked terrified. I wanted to hold her but she was pale, mouthing, 'Sorry, run... we've got to run.' She headed out the back door but they were clambering over the fence. She bolted the door fast. At the front window there were angry faces, blistered and reddened by the sun. Sue, Graham, even Father Hoare was there, egging them on.

We could see that they were burning up in the heat. The tarmac bent and collapsed under their weight but they refused to move, instead trying to see what food we had stored inside. A smash came from the back. Mum screamed.

We grabbed our bikes. Opened the side door — and hurtled outside. A lookout saw us and yelled. I pedalled and pedalled. I was cycling as fast as I could. The smell of melting rubber stung my eyes. I could taste it in on my tongue. I threw the bike down and turned to tell Mum to do the same, but I couldn't see her anywhere. I hopped from foot to foot. The ground hurt my feet. I fanned my face with my hands. The sun scorched my ears. I grew desperate. I waited for her to appear around the corner— but I knew she wasn't going to come.

I made my way to the river. Running. Then walking. Running then walking. It was hard to breathe. I ran faster. Tried to run faster still. Then the mob went quiet. It all stopped. I slowed to a jog. From the bank I saw people pour from their houses. I began to walk, watching the dusty ground freckle with rain.

Now I am sitting by the bridge. The rain is driving down. I remove my shoes. Let my feet swim in the water. I push my toes into the yielding ground. Enjoy the sludgey mud slipping through my fingers. I am on my knees now, digging with my hands. I make a pool of water. Rub the wet soil over my skin. Then I see bones. Small bones like those of child. I am thinking of Mum when I hear someone calling my name.

Digging Deep

RAMSEY CAMPBELL

It must have been quite a nightmare. It was apparently enough to make Coe drag the quilt around him, since he feels more than a sheeted mattress beneath him, and to leave a sense of suffocating helplessness, of being worse than alone in the dark. He isn't helpless. Even if his fit of rage blotted out his senses, it must have persuaded the family. They've brought him home. There wasn't a quilt on his hospital bed.

Who's in the house with him? Perhaps they all are, to impress on him how much they care about him, but he knows how recently they started. There was barely space for all of them around his bed in the private room. Whenever they thought he was asleep some of them would begin whispering. He's sure he overheard plans for his funeral. Now they appear to have left him by himself, and yet he feels hemmed in. Is the dark oppressing him? He has never seen it so dark.

It doesn't feel like his bedroom. He has always been able to distinguish the familiar surroundings when any of his fears jerked him awake. He could think that someone – his daughter Simone or son Daniel, most likely – has denied him light to pay him back for having spent too much of their legacy on the private room. However much he widens his eyes, they remain coated with blackness. He parts his dry lips to call someone to open the curtains, and then his tongue retreats behind his teeth. He should deal with the bedclothes first. Nobody ought to see him laid out as if he's awaiting examination. In the throes of the nightmare he has pulled the entire quilt under him.

He grasps a handful and plants his other hand against the padded headboard to lift his body while he snatches the quilt from beneath him. That's the plan, but he's unable to take hold of the material. It's more slippery than it ought to be, and doesn't budge. Did his last bout of rage leave him so enfeebled, or is his weight pinning down the quilt? He stretches out his arms to find the edges, and his knuckles bump into cushions on both sides of him. But they aren't cushions, they're walls.

He's in some kind of outsize cot. The walls must be cutting off the light. Presumably the idea is to prevent him from rolling out of bed. He's furious at being treated like this, especially when he wasn't consulted. He flings up his hands to grab the tops of the walls and heave himself up to shout for whoever's in the house, and his fingertips collide with a padded surface.

The sides of the cot must bend inwards at the top, that's all. His trembling hands have flinched and bruised his sunken cheeks, but he lifts them. His elbows are still pressed against the bottom of the container when his hands blunder against an obstruction above his face. It's plump and slippery, and scrabbling at it only loosens his nails from the quick. His knees rear up, knocking together before they bump into the obstacle, and then his feet deal it a few shaky kicks. Far too soon his fury is exhausted, and he lies inert as though the blackness is earth that's weighing on him. It isn't far removed. His family cared about him even less than he suspected. They've consigned him to his last and worst fear.

Can't this be another nightmare? How can it make sense? However prematurely eager Simone's husband may have been to sign the death certificate, Daniel would have had to be less than professional too. Could he have saved on the embalming and had the funeral at once? At least he has dressed his father in a suit, but the pockets feel empty as death.

Coe can't be sure until he tries them all. His quivering fists are clenched next to his face, but he forces them open and gropes over his ribs. His inside breast pocket is flat as a card, and so are the others in the jacket. When he fumbles at his trousers pockets he's dismayed to find how thin he is – so scrawny that he's afraid the protrusion on his right hip is a broken bone. But it's in the pocket, and in his haste to carry it to his face he almost shies it out of reach. Somebody cared after all. He pokes at the keypad, and before his heart has time to beat, the mobile phone lights up.

He could almost wish the glow it sheds were dimmer. It shows him how closely he's boxed in by the quilted surface. It's less than a hand's breadth from his shoulders, and when he tilts his face up to judge the extent of his prison the pudgy lid bumps his forehead. Around the phone the silky padding glimmers green, while farther down the box it's whitish like another species of mould, and beyond his feet it's black as soil. He lets his head sink onto the pillow that's the entire floor and does his desperate best to be aware of nothing but the mobile. It's his lifeline, and he needn't panic because he can't remember a single number. The phone will remember for him.

His knuckles dig into the underside of the lid as he holds the mobile away from his face. It's still too close; the digits merge into a watery blur. He only has to locate the key for the stored numbers, and he jabs it hard enough to bruise his fingertip. The symbol that appears in the illuminated window looks shapeless as a blob of mud, but he knows it represents an address book. He pokes the topmost left-hand key of the numeric pad, although he has begun to regret making Daniel number one, and holds the mobile against his ear.

There's silence except for a hiss of static that sounds too

much like a trickle of earth. Though his prison seems oppressively hot, he shivers at the possibility that he may be too far underground for the phone to work. He wriggles onto his side to bring the mobile a few inches closer to the surface, but before his shoulder is anything like vertical it thumps the lid. As he strives to maintain his position, the distant phone starts to ring.

It continues when he risks sinking back, but that's all. He's close to pleading, although he doesn't know with whom, by the time the shrill insistent pulse is interrupted. The voice isn't Daniel's. It's entirely anonymous, and informs Coe that the person he's calling isn't available. It confirms Daniel's number in a different voice that sounds less than human, an assemblage of digits pronounced by a computer, and invites him to leave a message.

'It's your father. That's right, I'm alive. You've buried me alive. Are you there? Can you hear me? Answer the phone, you — Just answer. Tell me that you're coming. Ring when you get this. Come and let me out. Come now.'

Was it his breath that made the glow flicker? He's desperately tempted to keep talking until this chivvies out a response, but he mustn't waste the battery. He ends the call and thumbs the key next to Daniel's. It's supposed to contact Simone, but it triggers the same recorded voice.

He could almost imagine that it's a cruel joke, even when the voice composed of fragments reads out her number. At first he doesn't speak when the message concludes with a beep, and then he's afraid of losing the connection. 'It's me,' he babbles. 'Yes, your father. Someone was a bit too happy to see me off. Aren't you there either, or are you scared to speak up? Are you all out celebrating? Don't let me spoil the party. Just send someone who can dig me up.'

He's growing hysterical. These aren't the sorts of comments he should leave; he can't afford to antagonise his family just now. His unwieldy fingers have already terminated the call – surely the mobile hasn't lost contact by itself. Should he ring his son and daughter back? Alternatively there are friends he could phone, if he can remember their numbers – and then he realises there's only one call he should make. Why did he spend so long in trying to reach his family? He uses a finger to count down the blurred keypad and jabs the ninth key thrice.

He has scarcely lowered the phone to his ear when an operator cuts off the bell. 'Emergency,' she declares.

Coe can be as fast as that. 'Police,' he says while she's enquiring which service he requires, but she carries on with her script. 'Police,' he says louder and harsher.

This earns him a silence that feels stuffed with padding. She can't expect callers who are in danger to be polite, but he's anxious to apologise in case she can hear. Before he can take a breath a male voice says 'Gloucestershire Constabulary.'

'Can you help me? You may have trouble believing this, but I'm buried alive.'

He sounds altogether too contrite. He nearly emits a wild laugh at the idea of seeking the appropriate tone for the situation, but the policeman is asking 'What is your name, sir?'

'Alan Coe,' says Coe and is pinioned by realising that it must be carved on a stone at least six feet above him.

'And where are you calling from?'

The question seems to emphasise the sickly greenish glimmer of the fattened walls and lid. Does the policeman want the mobile number? That's the answer Coe gives him. 'And what is your location, sir?' the voice crackles in his ear.

Coe has the sudden ghastly notion that his children haven't simply rushed the funeral – that for reasons he's afraid to contemplate, they've laid him to rest somewhere other than with his wife. Surely some of the family would have opposed them. 'Mercy Hill,' he has to believe.

'I didn't catch that, sir.'

Is the mobile running out of power? 'Mercy Hill,' he shouts so loud that the dim glow appears to quiver.

'Whereabouts on Mercy Hill?'

Every question renders his surroundings more substantial, and the replies he has to give are worse. 'Down in front of the church,' he's barely able to acknowledge. 'Eighth row, no, ninth, I think. Left of the avenue.'

There's no audible response. The policeman must be typing the details, unless he's writing them down. 'How long will you be?' Coe is more than concerned to learn. 'I don't know how much air I've got. Not much.'

'You're telling us you're buried alive in a graveyard.'

Has the policeman raised his voice because the connection is weak? 'That's what I said,' Coe says as loud.

'I suggest you get off the phone now, sir.'

'You haven't told me how soon you can be here.'

'You'd better hope we haven't time to be. We've had enough Halloween pranks for one year.'

Coe feels faint and breathless, which is dismayingly like suffocation, but he manages to articulate, 'You think I'm playing a joke.'

'I'd use another word for it. I advise you to give it up immediately, and that voice you're putting on as well.'

'I'm putting nothing on. Can't you hear I'm deadly serious? You're using up my air, you — Just do your job or let me speak to your superior.'

'I warn you, sir, we can trace this call.'

'Do so. Come and get me,' Coe almost screams, but his voice grows flat. He's haranguing nobody except himself.

Has the connection failed, or did the policeman cut him off? Did he say enough to make them trace him? Perhaps he should switch off the mobile to conserve the battery, but he has no idea whether this would leave the phone impossible to trace. The thought of waiting in the dark without knowing whether help is on the way brings the walls and lid closer to rob him of breath. As he holds the phone at a cramped arm's length to poke the redial button, he sees the greenish light appear to tug the swollen ceiling down. When he snatches the mobile back to his ear the action seems to draw the lid closer still.

An operator responds at once. 'Police,' he begs as she finishes her first word. 'Police.'

Has she recognised him? The silence isn't telling. It emits a burst of static so fragmented that he's afraid the connection is breaking up, and then a voice says 'Gloucestershire Constabulary.'

For a distracted moment he thinks she's the operator. Surely a policewoman will be more sympathetic than her colleague. 'It's Alan Coe again,' Coe says with all the authority he can summon up. 'I promise you this is no joke. They've buried me because they must have thought I'd passed on. I've already called you once but I wasn't informed what's happening. May I assume somebody is on their way?'

How much air has all that taken? He's holding his breath as if this may compensate, although it makes the walls and lid appear to bulge towards him, when the policewoman says in the distance, 'He's back. I see what you meant about the voice.'

'What's wrong with it?' Coe says through his bared teeth, then tries a shout, which sounds flattened by padding. 'What's the matter with my voice?'

'He wants to know what's wrong with his voice.'

'So you heard me the first time.' Perhaps he shouldn't address her as if she's a child, but he's unable to moderate his tone. 'What are you saying about my voice?'

'I don't know how old you're trying to sound, but nobody's that old and still alive.'

'I'm old enough to be your father, so do as you're told.' She either doesn't hear this or ignores it, but he ensures she hears, 'I'm old enough for them to pass me off as dead.'

'And bury you.'

'That's what I've already told you and your colleague.'

'In a grave.'

'On Mercy Hill below the church. Halfway along the ninth row down, to the left of the avenue.'

He can almost see the trench and his own hand dropping a fistful of earth into the depths that harboured his wife's coffin. All at once he's intensely aware that it must be under him. He might have wanted to be reunited with her at the end – at least, with her as she was before she stopped recognising him and grew unrecognisable, little more than a skeleton with an infant's mind – but not like this. He remembers the spadefuls of earth piling up on her coffin and realises that now they're on top of him. 'And you're expecting us to have it dug up,' the policewoman says.

'Can't you do it yourselves?' Since this is hardly the best time to criticise their methods, he adds, 'Have you got someone?'

'How long do you plan to carry on with this? Do you honestly think you're taking us in?'

'I'm not trying to. For the love of God, it's the truth.' Coe's free hand claws at the wall as if this may communicate his plight somehow, and his fingers wince as though they've scratched a blackboard. 'Why won't you believe me?' he pleads.

'You really expect us to believe a phone would work down there.'

'Yes, because it is.'

'I an't hea ou.'

The connection is faltering. He nearly accuses her of having wished this on him. 'I said it is,' he cries.

'Very unny.' Yet more distantly she says 'Now he's aking it ound a if it's aking up.'

Is the light growing unreliable too? For a blink the

darkness seems to surge at him – just darkness, not soil spilling into his prison. Or has his consciousness begun to gutter for lack of air? 'It is,' he gasps. 'Tell me they're coming to find me.'

'You won't like it if they do.'

At least her voice is whole again, and surely his must be. 'You still think I'm joking. Why would I joke about something like this at my age, for God's sake? I didn't even know it was Halloween.'

'You're saying you don't know what you just said you know.'

'Because your colleague told me. I don't know how long I've been here,' he realises aloud, and the light dims as if to suggest how much air he may have unconsciously used up.

'Long enough. We'd have to give you full marks for persistence. Are you in a cupboard, by the way? It sounds like one. Your trick nearly worked.'

'It's a coffin, God help me. Can't you hear that?' Coe cries and scrapes his nails across the underside of the lid.

Perhaps the squealing is more tangible than audible. He's holding the mobile towards it, but when he returns the phone to his ear the policewoman says, 'I've heard all I want to, I think.'

'Are you still calling me a liar?' He should have demanded to speak to whoever's in charge. He's about to do so when a thought ambushes him. 'If you really think I am,' he blurts, 'why are you talking to me?'

At once he knows. However demeaning it is to be taken for a criminal, that's unimportant if they're locating him. He'll talk for as long as she needs to keep him talking. He's opening his mouth to rant when he hears a man say, 'No joy, I'm afraid. Can't trace it.'

If Coe is too far underground, how is he able to phone? The policewoman brings him to the edge of panic. 'Count yourself lucky,' she tells him, 'and don't dare play a trick like this again. Don't you realise you may be tying up a line while someone genuinely needs our help?'

He mustn't let her go. He's terrified that if she rings off they won't accept his calls. It doesn't matter what he says so long as it makes the police come for him. Before she has finished lecturing him he shouts, 'Don't you speak to me like that, you stupid cow.'

'I'm war ing ou, ir – '

'Do the work we're paying you to do, and that means the whole shiftless lot of you. You're too fond of finding excuses not to help the public, you damned lazy swine.' He's no longer shouting just to be heard. 'You weren't much help with my wife, were you? You were worse than useless when she was wandering the streets not knowing where she was. And you were a joke when she started chasing me round the house because she'd forgotten who I was and thought I'd broken in. That's right, you're the bloody joke, not me. She nearly killed me with a kitchen knife. Now get on with your job for a change, you pathetic wretched – '

Without bothering to flicker the light goes out, and he hears nothing but death in his ear. He clutches the mobile and shakes it and pokes blindly at the keys, none of which brings him a sound except for the lifeless clacking of plastic or provides the least relief from the unutterable blackness. At last he's overcome by exhaustion or despair or both. His arms drop to his sides, and the phone slips out of his hand.

Perhaps it's the lack of air, but he feels as if he may soon be resigned to lying where he is. Shutting his eyes takes him closer to sleep. The surface beneath him is comfortable enough, after all. He could fancy he's in bed, or is that mere fancy? Can't he have dreamed he wakened in his coffin and everything that followed? Why, he has managed to drag the quilt under himself, which is how the nightmare began. He's vowing that it won't recur when a huge buzzing insect crawls against his hand.

He jerks away from it, and his scalp collides with the headboard, which is too plump. The insect isn't only buzzing, it's glowing feebly. It's the mobile, which has regained sufficient energy to vibrate. As he grabs it, the decaying light seems to fatten the interior of the coffin. He jabs the key to take the call and fumbles the mobile against his ear. 'Hello?' he pleads.

'Coming.'

It's barely a voice. It sounds as unnatural as the numbers in the answering messages did, and at least as close to falling to bits. Surely that's the fault of the connection. Before he can speak again the darkness caves in on him, and he's holding an inert lump of plastic against his ear.

There's a sound, however. It's muffled but growing more audible. He prays that he's recognising it, and then he's sure he does. Someone is digging towards him.

'I'm here,' he cries and claps a bony hand against his withered lips. He shouldn't waste whatever air is left, especially when he's beginning to feel it's as scarce as light down here. It seems unlikely that he would even have been heard. Why is he wishing he'd kept silent? He listens breathlessly to the scraping in the earth. How did the rescuers manage to dig down so far without his noticing? The activity inches closer – the sound of the shifting of earth – and all at once he's frantically jabbing at the keypad in the blackness. Any response from the world overhead might be welcome, any voice other than the one that called him. The digging is beneath him.

Mortal Coil

ROBERT SHEARMAN

On first impression, it looked like an apology. But the more you reread it – and it was reread a *lot* that day, it was pored over and analysed, governments around the world made statements about it, dismissing it first as a hoax, then taking it more seriously as the afternoon wore on, until by evening you could have sworn they had been in on the whole thing from the start, television programmes were rescheduled to make way for phone-in discussion shows and cobbled-together news reports that had very little actual news to report... The more you reread it, you couldn't help but feel there was a note of disappointment to it. It was almost patronising.

This is what the message said:

'You've got it all wrong. And we're sorry, because it's our mistake. If we'd made things clearer to you right from the start, none of this would have happened.

'We gave you a knowledge of death. We thought it would make you rise above the other animals, give you a greater perspective on how to live your lives fruitfully, in peace and in happiness. But it's all gone horribly wrong, hasn't it?

'You obsess about death. Right from childhood, it seems to exercise your imagination in an entirely unhealthy way. You count all the calories on every single tin in the supermarket, you go to the gym twice a week, just so you feel you can ward it off that bit longer. You pump Botox into your cheeks and stick plastic sacks into your breasts

so you can kid yourselves you look younger, that death isn't on the cards yet. And then, when death finally does happen, to someone you know, you go to long boring funerals and sit on hard benches in sullen silence, dressed in smart clothes that make you itch, with only flat wine and sausage rolls to look forward to. And the growing certainty that soon it'll be your turn, the sausage rolls will be eaten for you.

'You're frightened and you're miserable. We can't blame you. Looking down at you, it makes us pretty miserable too!

'Houseflies and worms and llamas have the right idea. They understand that death is just part of the system. As much as birth and procreation. A thing to avoid when it isn't necessary, and to accept when it is. And so houseflies and worms and llamas have a better grip on what's expected of them, to be as good houseflies, worms and llamas as they can be, and not let all that death baggage get in the way.

'As we say, sorry. We made the mistake of giving you a little knowledge, when either none or more would have been more sensible. There was some hope we didn't need to spell it all out for you, but don't you worry, that's our fault, not yours. And so we're going to put an end to it.

'We did consider that taking away the knowledge of death would be the best thing. But there was a general feeling that it'd be a shame to go backwards – and that we've enough houseflies and worms and llamas as it is. They're coming out our ears! So, starting tomorrow, expect things to be different. It'll be a new chapter. For you and for us!

'And in the mean time, please accept our apologies for any distress we may have caused you.'

You see, that patronising disappointment was hard to ignore. Especially after multiple readings of the message. Some very well-known intellectuals appeared on the phone-in discussion programmes that evening to complain that they'd been so obviously talked down to. 'After all,' grumbled one, 'what do they expect? If they're going to turn the secrets of life and death into a crossword puzzle, they can hardly object when we all sit around trying to solve it.'

The first message had naturally taken everyone by surprise. In every country around the world, on every television set, on every radio and in every newspaper, the words appeared. All in the language of the country in question, of course. Many people studied the different translations, just to see whether they could glean any hidden meanings, but all they could conclude was that (a) German words can be irritatingly long and never use one syllable when six will do, and that (b) French is very romantic. So no-one was any the wiser.

The next morning everyone was glued to their television screens. Even the sceptics, who stubbornly insisted the whole thing was some elaborate conjuring act, waited with bated breath to see what trickery was lined up next. And in countries where casual murder had become a part of everyone's daily lives, the perpetrators surprised themselves by holding back for once, and tuning in to see whether the killings they executed so nonchalantly had any deeper meaning. In Britain, the BBC didn't even bother to prepare their scheduled programmes. And so, when a second message resolutely *failed* to appear and explain life and death and matters besides, the BBC were caught on the hop and forced to transmit a series of Norman Wisdom films. Worldwide, the excitement gave way to disappointment, then to anger. It's quite certain there would have been riots in the streets, causing more bloodshed and more death, had Something Not Happened.

So it's just as well Something Did.

Of course, it took some people a while to realise anything had. They were so intent on the TV screen that they ignored the sound of the letterbox, of the daily post falling onto the mat. Had they stopped to consider that all the postmen were at home, the same as them, they might have shown more interest.

The envelopes were light brown, soft to the touch, and seemed almost to be made of vellum, like medieval manuscripts. There were no stamps on them – and the names weren't handwritten, but typed. And there was one for each member of the household, however young or old. Inside, each recipient found a card, stamped with his or her full name. And underneath that, as plain and unapologetic as you like, was a short account of when and how the recipient was going to die. Some poor unfortunates, either elderly or obese, found the news so startling that they died right there on the spot – and the card in their dead hands had predicted that exactly. Sometimes the explanation would be moderately chatty, and full of information. Arthur James Cripps learned that he was to die in fourteen years and six days, by 'drowning, after being knocked off a bridge by a Nissan Micra; frankly, if the water hadn't finished you off, you'd have died minutes later from the ruptured kidneys caused by the collision in question'. A lot of people learned that they were just going to die of 'cancer'. No fripperies, no more detail, no context – the word 'cancer' on the card saying it all, as if the typist had got so bored of hammering out the word so often that he could barely wait to move on to more interesting deaths elsewhere.

The Norman Wisdom films were interrupted, and news updates directed people to their letterboxes. The anticipation was terrible – worse than checking your exam results, or your credit card statement after a particularly expensive holiday. Parents with large families had to be put through the torture again and again, forced to confront what would happen not only to them but to their offspring. And if, inevitably, some were appalled by the bad news – a twelve year old child to die of meningitis, a three year old girl whose ultimate fate was to be abducted after school some seven years later, raped and strangled and her body never recovered — most went to bed that night somewhat reassured. At least they *knew* now. They might only have one month — one year — fifty years — but at least they *knew*. In fact, sales of cigarettes trebled almost overnight, as smokers and non-smokers alike realised that all the agonising over the health risks was now redundant. If it wasn't going to kill you, why not take it up? And if it was, well — it's a *fait accompli*, isn't it? Might as well enjoy it whilst your lungs last.

Just about the only person who wasn't reassured was Henry Peter Clifford.

Harry would never have thought he was an especially special person. Even in his moments of hubris or overweening arrogance — which, for him, were few and far between — he'd have been hard pushed to have described himself as anything better than distinctly average. He naturally assumed, on that fateful morning, that his envelope simply hadn't arrived yet. This was nothing new to Harry — his birthday cards were always late, he only received postcards after everybody else had had theirs. His wife Mary read her fate with shaking hands, and all he could think was that he'd probably have to wait until tomorrow to go through the same thing. But the next day there was still no envelope for him, nor the day after. The world had subtly changed, but for Harry it all looked pretty much the same.

The Government had quickly set up a number of help centres to deal with the crisis, and so, on the fourth day that Harry *still* hadn't found out when he was due to die, he caught the bus down to the citizens' advice bureau. The streets were that much more dangerous now; cars sped along roads knowing full well they *weren't* about to be involved in some tragic accident, and pedestrians ran the traffic with similar impunity. The bus driver catapulted his eight ton vehicle of red metal down the hill with the certain knowledge that his number wasn't up, and as Harry gripped the seat to prevent himself from being flung bodily down the aisle, he only wished he could be as sure.

There was a surprisingly long queue at the help centre, which cheered Harry somewhat – in spite of the long wait he'd have to put up with, it reassured him to think others were having complications too. But it turned out these people in line were just wanting grief counselling for deaths that hadn't even happened yet. Indeed, the rather bland blonde behind the desk suggested that Harry was the only person who *hadn't* received a death envelope.

'Well, what can I do about it?' asked Harry lamely, and she shrugged as if the oversight was in some way his fault. 'Is there anybody I can write to?' The woman told him that since no-one knew where the envelopes had come from there wasn't much she could do. 'But if you don't know anything about this whole thing, why have you set up a help centre?' The woman shrugged again, and called the next person in the queue forward.

'Maybe you just lost it somewhere?' said his secretary brightly. 'It fell behind the sofa cushions or something. I'm always doing that.' The secretary had been saying *everything* brightly after finding out that her death, in sixty-seven years' time, would be a painless little thing, her heart giving out in the throes of sexual congress with a South American toyboy. 'I should check under the cushions again,' she said, not a little unhelpfully.

The trouble was that everyone seemed to share his secretary's scepticism, and expressed it much less complacently. They were perplexed at first by Harry's outrageous claims he'd had no envelope, that he had been left out of a global miracle that had changed them all – as if he were the one man still claiming that the world was flat when everybody else had accepted it was a bloody sphere now, thank you very much. Then they'd get angry with the idea that he was trying to get attention. 'Why *wouldn't* you get an envelope? What makes you so special?' Typically, Harry hadn't thought of it in this way at all; on the contrary, he had wondered why the universe had deemed him so insignificant that he was the only one to be ignored. He vaguely mused whether he preferred the idea of being singled out because he was the most important person in the world, or because he was the *least* important. And decided he wasn't fond of either much, frankly.

'I'm afraid I'm going to have to let you go,' said his boss. 'You know, it's not my decision. But I have bosses, and they have bosses, and, you know…' He gave a smile. 'You know how it is.'

There had been some controversy about just how much employers had the right to know about their employees' life expectancy. Companies would argue that it was surely relevant whether or not they could expect their staff to go on providing good service, or whether they had to accommodate for the fact they might be dropping dead left, right and centre. At job interviews prospective employees lost out to candidates who could demonstrate they had longevity on their side, and those already in work found their bosses would rather ditch them quickly before they were subject to expensive health plans. The government said something non-committal about the data protection act and employee confidentiality, but also that any organisation had the right to expect full productivity from its staff. None of which helped anybody very much. When Harry was first asked to show his death envelope at work, his inability to do so was taken to mean he had something terrible and contagious and doubtlessly fatal to hide.

His boss gave him another one of those smiles. 'Really, you're lucky,' he said. 'Getting out of work is the best thing that can happen to you. Enjoy yourself. Enjoy the rest of your life. I wish I could,' he said with apparent regret, 'but it seems this old ticker of mine has another forty-seven years to go.

Bloody thing!' He held out his hand to wish Harry goodbye, and in spite of himself, Harry shook it.

And later that night his wife told him she was leaving.

'I can get another job,' said Harry. 'Nothing fancy, I know. But there's lots of casual labour, they don't care whether you snuff it or not. We can make it work, Mary.'

'No, we can't,' said Mary. And she told him how when she'd held that death envelope in her hand, scared to open it and find out how long she'd got, she'd made herself a vow. If I've only got a couple of years, she thought, if that's all I've got, then I'm out of here. I'm not going to waste any more of my life. Because we only go around once, and I'm letting it slip by. I should be climbing mountains and exploring deserts and scuba diving and sleeping with people who'd do it with the lights on. That'll be the present to myself. If I've got two years or less, I'm leaving Harry.

'But,' Harry pointed out gently, 'you haven't got two years. You've got thirty-eight. The cancer doesn't get you for thirty-eight.'

'I know,' said Mary. 'And I was so disappointed. And then it dawned on me. If I'm *that* disappointed, that I'd rather be dead than living with you, then I shouldn't be living with you. Goodbye, Harry.'

He couldn't argue with that.

Mary wasn't a cruel woman. She recognised that Harry wouldn't easily be able to earn money, whilst in her robust and not-yet-carcinogenic state the world was her oyster. She left him the house and a lot of the money. She also left him the cat, which Harry thought rather a shame as he'd never much liked it – he'd simply never got round to telling Mary that. And Mary said she wanted to start the rest of her life as soon as possible, and was gone by morning.

And, of course, a lot of people out there were following Mary's example. Those who realised that the end was in sight decided that this was their last chance to see the world.

Thousands of elderly English people flew to America, and thousands of elderly Americans flew to England – until, at the end of the day, roughly the same number of the diseased and the dying were roaming the streets in both countries, just sporting different accents. With typical brilliance, Disney decided to exploit this new trend in end-of-life tourism. They used a motto – 'Make the Last of Your Life be the Time of Your Life', which had a certain catchiness. If you could show proof you had three months or less, you were entitled to discounts to *all* the theme parks, and V.I.P. treatment once you were through the turnstiles. There was a special queue for the nearly dead, and a soberly dressed man-size Mickey Mouse or Goofy would respectfully show them to their rides. As it turns out the venture was so wildly successful that the Nearly Dead queue was often longer than the regular one, but that didn't matter – the ticket holders still felt they were being given special treatment. And attendance went up all the more when the elderly, who had always sworn that being spun through the air on a rollercoaster would be the death of them, now had concrete evidence that, in fact, it wouldn't.

Harry wouldn't have much wanted to visit Disneyland, but if his time were soon to be up, he'd certainly have wanted to have gone *somewhere*. But he couldn't afford a holiday. Unemployment benefits hadn't exactly been *abolished*, but it was hard to justify why you should be given a free hand-out when your death envelope demonstrated you had another fifty years of health in front of you and weren't just about to die in penury. And any attempt Harry made to get some money was thwarted by the absence of that envelope. So when, one morning, it came through the letterbox, Harry was delighted.

At first he couldn't believe it was really there. He'd given up hoping it'd ever turn up. But there was no mistaking it – that off-brown colour that you just didn't find anywhere else, the softness to the touch.

He opened it hastily. He didn't care *when* he died, or *how* he died. Just so long as he had proof he did, in fact, *eventually* die.

'**HENRY PETER CLIFFORD**', said the stamp.

And then, typed:

'Awaiting Further Information'.

Harry stared at it. Unable to believe his eyes. He turned over the card, hoping for something else. Something telling him it was a joke, not to worry, he was due to be impaled on a wooden stake that afternoon, anything. But instead, in ballpoint pen, someone had written, 'Sorry for the Inconveniance.'

As the day went by, as he did what he normally did – had breakfast, fed the cat, watched afternoon TV – Harry wondered whether the scrawled apology might even be God's very own handwriting. Still, probably not. He'd probably use one of his underlings, some saint or angel or vicar or someone. He'd always imagined the handwriting of a Divine Being would be a bit more ornate. And that he'd be able to spell 'inconvenience'.

The next morning he thought there might be another envelope, a follow-up to the last. There wasn't. But there was a knock at the door.

At first Harry saw the envelope rather than the man who was holding it. 'I think you should read this,' he said, and he held it out to Harry nervously.

Eagerly Harry read the name on the top, was immediately disappointed. 'Jeffrey Allan White. That isn't me.'

'No, it's me,' said Jeffrey Allan White.

'I don't understand,' said Harry. He held out the card for Mr White to take back. 'This isn't me,' he repeated uselessly.

'Please,' said Jeffrey. 'Read the rest of it.'

And Harry did. Then he read it again. He stared at Jeffrey for a few moments, and saw a man in his late fifties, a bit unkempt, shorter than average, plump, and just as scared as he was.

'Can I come in?' said Jeffrey. Harry nodded, and got out of his way.

Harry didn't know what to do with his strange visitor. He led him into the kitchen, wordlessly indicated he should sit down. Jeffrey smiled a thanks awkwardly. The cat was excited that someone new was in the house, and jumped up on to Jeffrey's lap. 'Sorry,' said Harry. 'Do you like cats...?'

'I'm a bit allergic,' replied Jeffrey. 'But it doesn't really matter any more.'

'Can I get you a drink?'

'I'm fine, thanks.'

'A coffee or a tea...?'

'A coffee then, thanks.'

'All I've got is decaf...'

'Decaf is fine.'

'Milk?'

'Yes. Thanks.' And there was silence from them both as Harry busied himself with the kettle. It wasn't until the water was nearly boiled that Harry thought he should say something.

'But I don't even know you.'

'No, I know.'

'But I don't. So why...?'

Jeffrey smiled, but it was a nervous smile that had no answer. 'Thanks,' he said as he took the coffee. 'Thanks, this is fine,' he said again.

'Why did you come here?' asked Harry. 'I mean, I'd have run away.'

'But really. Where would I go?'

Harry shrugged. 'Well. Anywhere.'

'I almost didn't come,' said Jeffrey quietly. 'When I first

found out how I was going to die… I almost laughed, it was so specific. My wife, she's one of the cancer ones, how can she avoid that? But if you know you're going to die at the hands of Henry Clifford at 23 Sycamore Gardens on 16th September, it seems such an easy thing to prevent. If you'd asked me last week,' he said, as he took a gulp of his still too hot coffee, 'I'd have said this was the last place in the world I'd have visited.'

Harry waited patiently for Jeffrey to go on. Jeffrey couldn't meet his eyes, looked at the floor.

'But if it isn't *true*… if I *could* prevent it… then it's all meaningless, isn't it? Isn't it? I'm not sure I could go on like that. I'm not sure I could cope with tomorrow, when I'm not supposed to see tomorrow in the first place. What would it all be for? My son,' he added. 'My son and I never much got on, we hadn't spoken in years. Once he found out I was going to die, he got back in touch. We've been going to the pub. Chatting. Like friends. Not as family, but *friends*.' He looked up at Harry imploringly. 'You've got to help me. You've got to do this. It says…' and he fluttered the envelope at Harry weakly, 'it says you do here.'

'I don't know how to stab someone. I'm not sure I could go through with it.' Silence. 'I mean, it's the actual sticking it in… I think I could do it if I had to shoot you, you know, from a distance…'

'It says stabbing.'

'Yes, I know.'

They both finished their coffee.

'Maybe,' suggested Jeffrey at last, 'you could just hold the knife. And I could run on to it.'

'Okay,' said Harry. 'We could try that.'

Both Harry and Jeffrey were shaking as Harry pulled open the kitchen drawer and looked at the knives. 'Do you have a preference, or…?'

'Best get one that's sharp,' said Jeffrey.

The first time Jeffrey ran at Harry's knife, Jeffrey kept his eyes closed. The problem was that Harry did the same. And so they didn't collide correctly, and the worst Jeffrey sustained was a cut on the arm.

'Ouch,' said Jeffrey.

'Sorry,' said Harry.

'There's no way that's fatal,' said Jeffrey. 'We should try again.'

This time Jeffrey, at least, kept his eyes open. Harry *tried* to, but at the moment of impact he couldn't help but flinch. So all he felt was Jeffrey's body groan against his, and a strange sucking as the knife was pulled out. When Harry dared to look, he was horrified to see there was blood everywhere, on his hands, on the floor, and on Jeffrey's stomach, of course, which was the point at which the knife had obviously entered.

'I'm sorry,' said Harry. 'I'm sorry. Does it hurt?'

Jeffrey laid on the floor, sobbing, clutching at his wound. 'Again,' he said. 'Again.'

Harry looked at all the blood, at Jeffrey's agonised face, and baulked. He left quickly, closing the kitchen door behind him.

An hour or so later he pushed the door open gently, as if trying not to wake his guest. 'Jeffrey,' he whispered. 'Are you still alive?'

'Please,' said Jeffrey, his voice now guttural. 'Finish me off.'

Harry stared. And then – 'No!' he said to the cat, as it poked its way into the kitchen, and began to lick at the blood with curiosity. 'Out of here, come on! Shoo! I'll close the door,' Harry said to Jeffrey gently. 'Leave you to it.'

Harry tried to watch the television, but it was hard to concentrate. Later that evening he went back to see how Jeffrey was holding up. Jeffrey couldn't speak, but looked at him with big desperate eyes. Harry hesitated. Then picked up a heavy rolling pin, stood over his victim, took aim at his head.

'No,' croaked Jeffrey. 'Stabbing. Says it's a stabbing.' And Harry left once more, determined to watch whatever was on the telly, and *make* himself concentrate on it.

Some time before midnight Harry braved the kitchen again. He was relieved to see that Jeffrey was, at last, dead. And had indeed died on the 16th September, even if the actual process had taken rather longer than either of them had anticipated. Harry looked at Jeffrey's eyes, as if trying to find some truth in his death, but all he saw was a glassy stare. He thought about moving the body, but realised that with all the worry he'd put into the actual killing, he'd not given a moment's thought to what he should do afterwards. And so he decided to go to bed, face that problem in the morning. After all, it wasn't as if Jeffrey Allan White was going anywhere.

That night Harry slept rather better than he thought any murderer had a right to – so soundly, in fact, that he was only woken up by frantic hammering at the door. He opened it in his pyjamas, so bleary that for the moment he forgot about the corpse on the kitchen floor.

Outside there were five people, each of them holding death envelopes.

'No,' he said. 'No, no, no.' And he closed the door on them.

But they didn't go away. They were staring death in the face, they were frightened – but each of them knew that their lives had to end somehow, and destiny had chosen them to be at the hands of Harry Clifford. The cat was very excited when he showed them all, one by one, into the sitting room, and with heavy heart read the grisly instructions within their soft little brown envelopes. There were two drownings, which Harry conducted in the bath one after the other – only realising as he lugged the swollen corpses into Mary's bedroom afterwards how heavy bodies became when full of water. Another one had his head caved in with an electric iron, and since Mary had been the one to take charge of all the practical details in their marriage, it took Harry a full half hour to find the right cupboard in which she'd kept it. There was another stabbing to be performed, but this one was quicker than the day before's; Harry had learned to keep his eyes open this time. And there was a hanging, which caused both Harry and his victim no end of problems.

'Did you bring a rope?' asked Harry.

'I didn't know I needed one,' said the rather shy teenager, blushing through a wall of spots.

'I don't just have a rope lying about,' said Harry. 'If you want me to hang you, the least you could do is bring your own equipment.'

In the end they decided that the shower curtains could be taken down, wrapped tightly around the youth's neck, and with some care he could be suspended over the upstairs banisters until he expired. Then Harry cut the body down, dragged it to Mary's bedroom, and laid it alongside the five people he had already killed. Mary's room seemed the best place for all these strangers; it was a place he'd had little cause to visit over the last two years of his marriage, not since Mary had asked if he could move into the spare room. He surveyed his handiwork for a moment, all six bodies lying higgledy-piggledy across Mary's bed and by the dressing table at which she used to do her make-up and hair. Then, without hesitation, he closed the door tight, went to his own room, packed a rucksack, and left the house.

The next day he was on the Cornwall coast, walking along the cliffs, watching as the sea crashed into the rocks. He began to feel normal, human. He waved politely at the passers-by, managed a smile, as if he too was simply out for a gentle stroll without a care in the world. One kindly looking old man, walking his Jack Russell, said good morning.

'Good morning,' said Harry.

'Here on holiday?' asked the old man.

'Yes,' said Harry. 'I think so. I don't know. Maybe,' he said decisively, 'I'll live here. Yes.'

'Well, it's a beautiful part of the country. I've always loved it, man and boy. I say,' said the old man confidentially, 'I do believe you're supposed to push me off the cliff.' And he produced the telltale envelope. 'I'm sorry,' he said, with genuine sympathy. 'I can quite see how that would disturb your walk.'

Harry pushed him over the side, and his body spun all the way down, glancing off the odd rock. Neither of them had been quite sure what to do with the little dog, so the old man had kicked him off the edge before he took his own fall. 'He loved me, I know it,' he'd said with tears in his eyes. 'It's what he would have wanted.'

If these death envelopes were going to follow Harry wherever he went, he supposed he might as well go back home and live in comfort. The cat was pleased – he hadn't been fed for nearly a day, and was starving. And the people *did* keep coming. Sometimes as many as twenty could be found in the morning, sick with fear, clutching their little death sentences. 'It's all right,' he said to them, soothing, calm. 'We'll make it okay. There's nothing to be afraid of.' And, as the weeks went by, and the corpses began mounting in his ex-wife's bedroom, he realised that he meant it. All this death, there really *was* nothing to be afraid of. If he'd found a purpose in life, at long last, after so many years of not even bothering to look, then this was it – he could make sure that these poor souls shuffled off this mortal coil in as humane and tender a way as possible.

He decided to charge his victims a small fee. They were all too eager to pay, he discovered – it wasn't as if they could take their money with them. And with the cash he bought lots of painkillers, the strongest that could be purchased over the counter. When all's said and done, if your way out of this world is by having a hammer turn your skull to splinters, then a preparatory swig of a couple of aspirin is unlikely to do much good. But Harry realised it was a *psychological* help, that his patients felt it was altogether a far more professional operation. 'Thank you, doctor,' said one gratefully, just before Harry bludgeoned him with a saucepan, and Harry felt an indescribable swell of pride.

He even hired a secretary to take care of them all, to ensure that he disposed of them in order and in good time. He chose the secretary he'd once worked with, the one who so brightly had realised her death was at the thrust of a toyboy. She was no longer so bright or cheery. 'I've not even had a sniff of sex in ages,' she complained. 'What if this toyboy in sixty-seven years' time is the next bit of sex I get? It's a mistake,' she concluded, with a wisdom that Harry had never expected of her, 'to see in the way you die an explanation of how you live. The fact I'm going to die bonking a Brazilian does not mean I'm a great lover. Death is just another bit of stuff that happens.'

And then, one day, just suddenly, it all stopped.

'A quiet day today,' the secretary told Harry, when, by noon, no-one had knocked at the door. But it was a quiet week as well. At the end of the month, with no patients calling, Harry paid her off. She said she was sorry the job was over. 'I felt we were doing some good.' Harry told her he was sorry too.

But, surprisingly, sorrier still was the cat. The ginger little tabby had been a great favourite with all Harry's victims, taking their minds off the operations ahead of them. It'd enjoyed parading around the waiting room of a morning, checking out all the newcomers, and allowing itself to be stroked and petted and made a fuss of. Now the cat would stare out of the window, eyeing anyone who walked up the street — and visibly sagging with disappointment when the passer-by wouldn't stop at the house. The cat's fur grew matted and coarse, it no longer washed itself. It had no interest in eating, it had no interest in anything. It was beginning to pine away.

Harry could see his cat was dying. And it seemed to him an extraordinary piece of cruelty that he should never know exactly when the cat was to die, when its suffering was to stop. The cat would lie, listless, looking at him with pleading eyes. Harry recognised the look; it was the same expression he'd seen in Jeffrey White's when he'd bled to death in the kitchen all those months ago.

Harry cradled the cat in his arms, and stroked its fur. He'd never liked the cat, and the cat had never much liked him — but it purred for Harry now, and Harry was touched. The cat heaved with a huge sigh that seemed to echo down its thinning body, and then gave the gentlest of mews. And Harry knew there was no person more humane than him to end the poor cat's life, and that the cat knew it too, he'd seen the fact of it countless times in this very house. Because Harry was the greatest killer of all, and he *was* special, and that's why he'd been singled out, that's why he couldn't die, why they wouldn't let him die, he had a job to do. He wringed the cat's neck, so quickly the cat would never have known. And he carried its frail little body up to Mary's room, and left it with all the other corpses.

And then he sat down and cried. He hadn't cried for any of these deaths, he hadn't found the time. But he cried now, and he cried himself asleep.

The next morning he started when he heard something at the door. Still dozing in the armchair, he sprang to his feet. Ready to welcome another client, to practise his expertise with gentle care.

But instead, lying on the doormat, was an off-brown envelope.

Numbly he picked it up. And opened it. And read it.

'**HENRY PETER CLIFFORD**' said the stamp.

And, underneath, just the one word:

'Cancer'.

And that was it. Not even a date. Not even the recognition that there should have been a date. Just this one word, this ordinary death, this trivial death, laughing at him.

He turned over the card. And, in the same handwriting he'd seen before, in ballpoint pen: 'Sorry. We lost this behind the sofa cushion.'

Harry sighed. He put the card back in the envelope for safe keeping, laid it gently down upon the hall table. He wondered what he should do with the rest of the day, the rest of his life. He couldn't think of anything.

So he went upstairs to bed. Drew the curtains. And, lying in the darkness, explored his body for a lump.

Contributors

Chaz Brenchley has been making a living as a writer since he was eighteen. He is the author of nine thrillers, most recently *Shelter*, and two major fantasy series; his most recent book is *Bridge of Dreams*. His novel *Light Errant* won the British Fantasy Award in 1998. He lives in Newcastle upon Tyne with a quantum cat and a famous teddy bear.

Ramsey Campbell is described by *The Oxford Companion to English Literature* as 'Britain's most respected living horror writer.' His many award-winning novels include *The Face That Must Die, Incarnate,* and most recently *The Overnight* (PS Publishing). He reviews regularly for BBC Radio Merseyside.

Paul Cornell is the author of eight science fiction novels. He also works prolifically as a screenwriter, writing for BBC TV's *Doctor Who* (where he created of one of the Doctor's spin-off companions, *Bernice Summerfield*), and for a host of other popular drama series on British television, including *Casualty, Holby City, Coronation Street* and *Robin Hood*.

Frank Cottrell Boyce is a novelist and screenwriter. His film credits include *Welcome to Sarajevo, Hilary and Jackie, 24 Hour Party People* and *A Cock and Bull Story*. In 2004, his debut novel *Millions* won the Carnegie Medal and was shortlisted for

The Guardian Children's Fiction Award. His second novel, *Framed*, was published by Macmillan in 2005.

Jeremy Dyson is an award-winning writer for television (*Funland* and the Bafta Award-winning *League of Gentlemen*), director (*Cicerones*), novelist (*What Happens Now*, Abacus), and short story writer (*Never Trust a Rabbit*, Duck Editions). A recent story, 'Michael', featured in *The Book of Leeds* (Comma, 2006).

Matthew Holness was educated at Trinity Hall, Cambridge and was vice-president of the Cambridge Footlights Dramatic Club 1995-1996. He won the Perrier Comedy Award in 2001 for Garth Marenghi's Netherhead, and has since appeared in *The Office, Casanova,* and his own Channel 4 television series *Garth Marenghi's Darkplace* and *Man to Man With Dean Learner.*

Hanif Kureishi's first play, *Soaking the Heat*, was performed at the Royal Court Theatre in London in 1976. Since then he has enjoyed success as a playwright, screenwriter, novelist and short story writer. His first novel, *The Buddha of Suburbia*, was published in 1990 to widespread acclaim, and won the Whitbread First Novel Award. He has published also three collections of short stories: *Love in a Blue Time, Midnight All Day* and *The Body and Other Stories.*

Paul Magrs has written novels and short stories for adults, teens, children and Doctor Who fans. His latest novel is the comic Gothic mystery, *Never the Bride*, published by Headline. He teaches Creative Writing at Manchester Metropolitan University.

Andy Murray has worked as a film reviewer for Manchester's *City Life* and the website www.kamera.co.uk.

Since graduating with an MA in Scriptwriting from Salford University, he's collaborated on several short films, and written a biography of legendary scripter Nigel Kneale for Headpress. His stories have appeared in Comma's *Manchester Stories* series and *Parenthesis* (2006). He is currently working on an academic study of TV writer Russell T Davies.

Lavinia Murray writes scripts. Her last short film was shown at a Texan Splatterfest. She is writing a children's novel, and recently attended an open audition for a skincare commercial but was asked to leave when she refused to dance to 'I Will Survive' in her bra and knickers.

Christine Poulson had a career as an art historian before she turned to crime writing. She has written three novels set in Cambridge, featuring academic turned amateur detective, Cassandra James, the most recent being *Footfall*. She has also written widely on nineteenth century art and literature and is a research fellow in the Department of Nineteenth Century Studies at the University of Sheffield.

Maria Roberts was born in 1977 in Manchester. She studied English and Spanish at the University of Manchester and has just graduated from the Creative Writing School at MMU. She has previously published a short story in *Bracket* (Comma, 2004), and her play *White Wedding* was produced by 24:7 Theatre in 2005.

Nicholas Royle is the author of five novels – *Counterparts, Saxophone Dreams, The Matter of the Heart, The Director's Cut* and *Antwerp* – as well as one collection of short stories, *Mortality* (Serpent's Tail, 2006). He has edited twelve anthologies of short fiction including *A Book of Two Halves, The Tiger Garden: A Book of Writers' Dreams, The Time Out Book of New York Short Stories*, and *Dreams Never End* (Tindal Street Press).

Robert Shearman is currently best-known as a writer for *Doctor Who* as well as BBC drama *Born and Bred* and seven plays for BBC Radio 4. As a theatrical playwright, Shearman has worked with Alan Ayckbourn, had a play produced by Francis Ford Coppola, and has received several international awards for his work in theatre. His *Doctor Who* episode 'Dalek' was nominated for the Hugo Award for Best Dramatic Presentation, Short Form in 2006.

Emma Unsworth works as a journalist in Manchester. She mostly writes short stories, but is also in the process of finishing her first novel. She is scared of the dark and probably drinks too much.

Conrad Williams is the author of three novels: *Head Injuries, London Revenant* and *The Unblemished*: and three novellas: *Nearly People, Game* and *The Scalding Rooms*. In 2004 his first collection of short stories, *Use Once then Destroy*, was published by Night Shade Books. He is also a past recipient of the Littlewoods Arc Prize and the British Fantasy Award.